Love Signs

M. L. Kennedy

SCHOLASTIC INC.
New York Toronto London Auckland Sydney

For Gil,
the source of my best one-liners

ISBN 0-590-33268-6

12 11 10 9 8 7 6 5 4 3 2 1   5   5 6 7 8 9/8 0/9

Printed in the U.S.A.   06

A Wildfire Book

WILDFIRE® TITLES FROM SCHOLASTIC

$O^{\underline{ne}}$

I suppose it all began with the book.

It had a glossy red and black cover and it seemed to jump right off the library shelf at me. *Secrets of the Stars: A Beginner's Guide to Astrology.* Before I really knew what I was doing, I reached out and grabbed it.

"One more, Mrs. Adams," I told the school librarian.

She smiled at me. "That's six books on European history, two on the Crusaders, and . . . *Secrets of the Stars,*" she said, thoughtfully. "We just got that book in today. You're the first person to check it out."

"I should stick to the history books," I said, feeling a little silly. "I've got a term paper due on the Roman Empire, but. . . ."

"But you might want to take a break and read something for fun."

"Exactly. How did you guess?"

She leaned across the counter and grinned. "My birthday's November twenty-fifth."

I waited. "Should that mean something?"

"I can see you don't know your astrology, Tracy Evans." She grinned even wider. "I'm a Sagittarius, and we're amazingly perceptive. In fact, some people think that we can read minds."

"Really?" I was interested, and would have liked to talk to her some more, but someone nudged me sharply in the back with a notebook. It was almost closing time and all the kids were making a mad scramble for the checkout counter.

"Oh yes," she said enthusiastically. "You can almost always predict someone's personality once you know their sign."

"What's my sign?" I asked quickly. The corner of the notebook was grinding its way into my shoulder blade.

"Birthday?" she said crisply.

"I was sixteen on February twenty-eighth."

"You're a Pisces." She seemed pleased with herself. "I guessed it the moment you walked in here."

"Is that good or bad? To be a Pisces, I mean."

"Oh, it's good, Tracy. Your sign is the fish. We'll talk more next time," she promised. She handed me my books and the line surged forward.

I walked away from the counter feeling vaguely disappointed. Pisces — a fish! It was hardly an exciting prospect. What did it all mean? I was dying to sneak a look at the astrology book, but I knew I'd have to tackle the Roman Empire first.

The house was quiet when I got home, except for the gentle hum of the computer. My seventeen-year-old brother, Tom, is a "hacker," which means he lives, breathes, and probably dreams computers. He hardly ever bothers to talk to anyone when he's hunched over the keyboard, and I was surprised when he yelled to me from the dining room.

"Hey, Tracy," he called. "Come on in here for a minute."

I dropped my books on the hall table and flipped through the mail. Four computer ads and an electric bill. Fascinating.

"What's up?" I said. The dining room was a mess. Tom keeps the computer keyboard and screen on the sideboard, but there were disks and paper and notebooks spread all over the table. Mom tries to make the room cozy with hanging plants and dried flowers, but it's a lost cause. I always feel like I'm walking into Radio Shack.

"Ricky brought over his voice synthesizer. You're not gonna believe the stuff it can do!" His voice was excited, and I tried not to smile. Tom always thinks that people find computers as fascinating as he does.

"Mmm," I said noncommittally.

"Oh, Rick, this is my sister, Tracy. Rick

Jacobs." Rick nodded, and I sighed and sat down. It was obvious I'd never escape without seeing the latest computer marvel.

"Uh, Tom, I really have to get started on my term paper. . . ."

"This will only take a minute," he said, jumping up and thumbing through a box of disks. "Wait till you hear this. It'll blow you away. Rick, why don't you do the honors?"

Rick smiled at me and hit some keys. "Okay, Tracy, listen to this." He pressed a button, and I heard a squeaky, electronic voice. It was impossible to make out what it was saying.

"Well?" He paused expectantly.

I glanced at Tom. "What was it?"

"Didn't you hear it?" he said impatiently. "Play it again for her, Rick. And this time, listen!"

I squinted and closed my eyes.

"Did you get it?" Rick and Tom were staring at me, and I tried not to giggle.

"It sounds like a little electronic man . . ."

"Yes . . ."

"Talking in a toilet."

"Tracy. . . ." Tom said threateningly.

The voice came on again. "Wait, I think I get it," I said finally. "It's saying: Ah . . . tra . . . see. Atrocity? Is that it?"

They gave me a disgusted look. "It said, 'Hi, Tracy,'" Rick said.

"Sorry about that." I grinned and stood up. "I'm just not into computers, guys."

I was pouring myself a glass of milk in the

kitchen a few minutes later when Tom came up behind me. "He really likes you, you know."

I was mystified. "Who?" I said, trying to balance four fudge brownies and the milk all on one plate.

"Rick," he said, lowering his voice. "In fact, he'd like to take you out."

"What!" I nearly dropped the plate.

"Be quiet, he'll hear you. He's a very shy guy, and he's afraid to ask you himself."

"You've got to be kidding."

"Why do you say that?"

"Tom, he's a —" I was going to say nerd, and caught myself. "He's just not my type." I secretly didn't see how he could be anybody's type, but I didn't want to make an issue of it.

"You'd have a great time together."

I pictured Rick behind the dining room door. Lank hair, horn-rimmed glasses, polyester shirt. Mr. Excitement, he wasn't.

"At least think about it," Tom pleaded.

"Mmm." I grabbed the plate in one hand, my notebook in the other and started upstairs to my room.

Tom followed me to the foot of the stairs. "Tracy, you're making a big mistake. He's one of the best hackers I know. And as far as games go, this guy got eighty-thousand on Space Invaders. Eighty-thousand!"

I sighed and gently nudged open the door to my room. Tom and I were complete opposites. How could we be so different when we were born to the same parents and lived in the same house? And we were even born in the same month. I decided to look up Tom's astrological sign after dinner. Maybe the stars could reveal some secrets to me, after all.

I was making a half-hearted attempt to follow Attila and his merry band of Huns through Europe when the phone rang.

"What are you up to?" It was Laura Kane. We've been best friends since third grade and make it a point to see each other, or at least talk to each other, every single day.

I told her what I was doing and she groaned. "You, too? I'm working on the Visigoths, and then I've got to start on another tribe, the Vandals. I've got a really neat theme for my paper, though. I'm comparing the barbarians to modern rock groups."

"What!" Laura gets some pretty far-out ideas, but this one was the worst.

"Yeah, it just sort of came to me," she said modestly. "I think Mr. Welsh will go for it. He's always telling us to come up with something original."

"But Laura," I protested, "I don't get it. The barbarians were awful. They looted and burned, and took everything that wasn't nailed down."

"Exactly. Just like rock stars on tour," she said eagerly. "Europe was just one big Holiday Inn to them. And think of all the groupies — that's worth a page and a half!"

I shuddered. "I suppose so," I said doubtfully. Laura wants to be a writer, and I certainly don't want to discourage her. She always says she's glad that I don't "throw water on the fires" of her "creative genius." So a lot of times, I bite my tongue and keep my opinions to myself.

"Laura, do you ever read your horoscope?" I asked suddenly.

"Sometimes. Why?"

"I don't know. I just wondered. You don't have a newspaper handy, do you? Tom's got a friend here, and I don't want to go downstairs to get ours."

She laughed. "I think it ended up in the cat box. Who's he got over there, anyway?"

"Rick Jacobs," I said in a low voice. "And worst of all . . . he wants to take me out!"

"Old Four Eyes himself! I don't believe it," she squealed.

"I have no intention of going," I assured her.

"I should hope not. Have you seen those Hawaiian shirts he wears? You'd think he was entering a Don Ho look-alike contest. And his hair — he must comb it with a fork!"

I laughed and hung up. If Laura decides not to be a writer, she can probably make it as a comedian.

I tuned out most of the dinner conversation, because I was still thinking about that astrology book. I wanted to tell Mom about it, but as usual Dad and Tom were monopolizing the conversation with computer talk.

"We got a new computer in at work today. It's got five-hundred and twelve K of memory and a hard disk drive."

Tom nearly dropped his meatball. "Man, you're lucky! I read about those in *Computer Finds* this month. It says they have a terminal emulation mode and a four-color plotter that's the best on the market."

"Really? I must have missed that article. Think you can dig it up for me after dinner?"

"Sure," Tom said happily. "And then maybe we can work the bugs out of that graphics program. You know, I think the first subroutine is causing the trouble."

"And we need to set up a sequential text file for the household budget. It's going to take a lot of time, though."

"That's okay, I did my homework after school. I've got all night."

Mom caught my eye and winked. She cares even less about computers than I do, and if you asked her what a floppy disk is, she'd probably say it was a pancake. When Dad and Tom wanted to reorganize all her recipes on the computer, she just laughed and said she liked keeping them stuffed in a drawer.

"Really, Tina," Dad had said, irritated. "It's so disorganized doing things that way. If everything was filed in the computer, you could find exactly what you need in a few seconds. It would even be cross-indexed."

"But then there wouldn't be any surprises," she explained seriously. "This way, I can hunt through the drawer for a meatloaf recipe and come across a recipe for sweet and sour pork that sounds much better. I like my own system the best," she said firmly.

"Mom, do you know what sign Tom was born under?" We were doing the dinner dishes while Dad and Tom were sitting mesmerized in front of the green screen.

"Sure I do. The same as your father."

"Really? They were born in different months."

"Well, they're both Aquarians," she said with a smile. "I remember the nurse in the hospital remarking on it. Why the sudden interest in astrology?"

"Oh, I don't know. I just happened to pick up a book on it, that's all." I paused. "You don't think there's really anything to it, do you?"

She dried her hands and turned to face me. The kitchen was very quiet, but we could hear shouts of laughter coming from the dining room. "Sometimes I wonder," she said wryly. "Tom and your father are so much alike that it's uncanny. Like two peas in a pod. I bet if you look up Aquarians in your book, you'll find that they're usually very scientific types. After all, Tom certainly didn't get his mathematical mind from me. You know how I feel about computers."

"You wouldn't want to spend an evening with one?" I teased.

"I'd rather have root canal work done,"

9

she said flatly. She laughed and sat down to read the paper. "But to answer your question, no, I don't think that your future could ever depend on what sign you were born under. Look, here's the horoscope section. This proves my point."

"Look at Pisces," I urged her.

She grinned and began reading. "A sudden change of plans can work to your advantage. . . ."

"That's right! My history test was canceled this morning," I said excitedly.

She stared at me and kept on. "But be prepared to meet the test in a day or two. . . ."

"That's true, too! It was rescheduled for Thursday." I could hardly believe it. The horoscope was practically written for me.

"Beware of false friends who try to take advantage of your good nature . . ." Kimberly Walker tried to copy my math homework, but I didn't want to tell Mom that.

". . . and don't be surprised if you hear from a voice in your past."

I had to admit that the part about a voice from the past didn't ring a bell, but I suppose horoscopes can't be right all the time. I'm sure there's a margin for error. We learned all about that when we studied statistics.

"You see, honey," Mom said. "They make these horoscopes so general, they'd fit anybody. They try to cover every possibility, so you're bound to find something that you think relates to you."

"I suppose you're right," I said, not convinced. "Well, it's back to my term paper," I said, getting up. "Twenty brilliant pages on the Roman Empire."

"And your horoscope didn't say a word about it," Mom said wryly. "That should tell you something."

I managed to put horoscopes and birth signs out of my mind, and actually made a good start on my paper. I didn't have a fascinating theme like Laura did, but I was sure I'd find something to write about. I was shuffling my index cards around when the phone rang. It was ten-thirty, which is a little late for someone to call.

I reached for the phone and gave a weary hello.

"Hi, Tracy," a cheery voice said. "This is a voice from your past."

I nearly dropped the phone. I tried to form a question, but no sound came out. I thought I recognized the soft giggle, but I couldn't be sure.

"It's me — Jenny. Your third grade pal, remember? We went on our first camping trip together."

Jenny! Of course I remembered. We were inseparable until her family moved to Oregon. "Jenny!" I blurted out, "What are you doing in town? It's been ages."

"It sure has," she agreed. "I'm only here for the night, and I'm really sorry to call so late. But I couldn't resist the urge to hear your voice."

"I'm glad you called," I said honestly. "I never expected to hear from you."

Or did I? I wondered. Wasn't that exactly what my horoscope had predicted? She even used the exact same words. *A voice from the past.*

I decided to read the astrology book the very next day. It was obvious that I had a lot to learn.

T*wo*

The next day was a disaster.

I overslept, and Mom stormed into my room like the gestapo at seven-thirty-five. "Look at this mess!" she said, stumbling over a pile of records. "Your room is like an obstacle course. There could be land mines buried under this rubble, and you wouldn't even know!" I thought the bit about land mines was a little far-fetched, but Mom was clearly on a roll.

She flung open the drapes so I could have a breathtaking view of gray skies and driving rain.

"Thanks a lot," I muttered, trying to burrow back into the pillow.

"I want you downstairs in ten minutes, young lady," she said in her best drill-sergeant voice. "And another thing . . ." I moaned, but she ignored me. "I want this room cleaned up after school, and I mean *cleaned up*!" She turned to the door, tripped over a stuffed panda, and gave it a swift kick.

I could hardly wait to run downstairs and have breakfast.

"Don't let your eggs get cold," Mom said crisply. Mom is one of those people who thinks that breakfast is the most important meal of the day. At least for other people. She always put out enough food for a gang of stevedores, and then she nibbles on half a slice of diet toast.

I watched Tom, fascinated. He's so neat and methodical he drives me crazy. Ever since he was a little kid, he's had this crazy habit of cleaning his plate — one item at a time. Every morning, he starts with a glass of orange juice. Then he eats all the eggs, then the bacon, then the blueberry muffins. He never mixes anything up. If you tried to make him eat something out of sequence, he'd probably starve to death. It's like he was programmed . . . just like his computer, I thought suddenly. A true Aquarius, I bet.

I thought of the astrology book lying upstairs on my nighttable. If everything went okay, I'd be able to start reading it in study hall.

Just when you think things can't get any worse, they invariably do. My umbrella blew inside out on the way to school, and I got soaked to the skin. A quick glance in the mirror confirmed the worst.

"Hi," Laura said, peering in the mirror at me. "Gosh, I've got to hurry. The first bell is going to ring any second." We were alone in the girl's bathroom. "I don't know if I should go with brown eyeshadow in the crease, or just stick to blue like I usualy do. What do you think?"

I looked at her and sighed. If she wasn't my best friend, it would be very easy to be jealous of Laura. She's one of those rare, lucky people who always looks good with no apparent effort. She has green eyes and a beautiful smile. And most annoying of all, she has straight blonde hair that falls to her shoulders. Mine is naturally wavy dark blonde and everyone tells me how lucky I am, but I've always wanted hair like Laura's.

"Well, which do you think?" she said. "Brown or blue? Or maybe both," she added, biting her lower lip. She turned and stared at me. "Aren't you even going to put on some lipstick, Tracy. I know you don't like makeup, but without lipstick, you'll look like a zombie."

"I'll look like a zombie?" I smiled at her and then stopped. "What do you mean?"

"The class pictures," she said irritably. "Today's the day, you know."

I remembered a line from a romance book I had read. The heroine had felt "icy fingers grip her heart." I had laughed at the time, thinking what a silly image it was. Now I knew differently. Not only were the fingers gripping my heart, they were running up and down my spine like it was a piano keyboard.

"I can't believe you forgot." She added some lip gloss and stood back to study the effect.

"I can't either," I said weakly. I stared at the pale face and wild hair in the mirror and wanted to hide. There must be some way out! My mind groped wildly for an excuse. "I know! I'll get sick. I'll just pretend to be sick and then I can go home. . . ."

"Not on frog day you won't," Laura said calmly. "You know what Mr. Giandi said. If anyone misses the frog finals, they have to start over with a new frog."

The frog finals! It sounded like some new kind of animal Olympics. If I hadn't felt so depressed, I would have burst out laughing. Laura was right, though. There was no way I could miss frog day. We had been dissecting "Kermit" for over three weeks now, and today was the day that we'd get our grades.

"You seem to be forgetting a lot of things lately," Laura said. "First the pictures, and now frog day."

"Maybe it's just not my day," I muttered. I looked in the mirror again. I had worn my oldest, most frayed sweater, which didn't help. It was hopeless. "What am I going to do?" I wailed. "I look a wreck — my hair, my skin, my clothes. . . ."

Laura looked at me sympathetically. "You do look a little pale." She was doing her best to be diplomatic. I have the kind of white skin that often goes with fair hair. Sometimes it looks like fine porcelain, and sometimes it looks like a bad embalming job. Today I looked like I had just risen from the grave.

"Well, it's hopeless," I said miserably. "I can't cancel out on the pictures, and I can't do anything to look better. So unless you have any suggestions. . . ."

"I'm afraid not," she said, giving a final pat to her gleaming blonde hair. She giggled suddenly. "Unless. . . ." She started laughing and couldn't continue.

"Unless what?" I was beginning to feel a little annoyed.

"Unless you want to wear a paper bag over your head!" She chuckled and darted out the door just as the bell rang.

"It's either a tongue or a gall bladder," Laura said thoughtfully. Her hair fell over one eye and she made a swipe at something with the dissecting knife.

"Laura, that's impossible. They're miles apart!" Laura and I never should have been paired together in biology lab. Laura is too reckless to dissect things, and I get queasy at the smell of formaldehyde.

"Well, don't blame me," she said, annoyed. "This stupid frog doesn't even look like the one they have in the book. Nothing's in the right place. And I think he's missing half his insides, anyway. No wonder he never made it past puberty. Look, he doesn't have a heart." She stuck the probe angrily in Kermit's chest.

"Laura," I said mildly, "it's right there. Three chambers, see? Two atria and one ventricle. You better remember that. I'm sure Mr. Giandi will ask about the heart."

"You're probably right." She sighed and glanced at her watch. "We've only got another hour to label this stuff. Why don't you read the list and then maybe we can see what we're missing."

"Small intestine . . . large intestine . . . pancreas. . . . Do we have that?" Laura shuddered and speared something slimey. "That's it," she said, making a face. "He seems to have an extra liver, though. I wonder if that matters?" She laughed. "Maybe he's some kind of mutant. Like a frog from another planet."

"His liver is supposed to look like that," a male voice said. "It has three lobes."

I spun around to face Jeff Nichols. Jeff is a really great-looking guy who joined our class a few weeks ago. His family is new in town, and nobody knows him very well.

"How do you know that?" Laura countered.

"Maybe he's known a lot of frogs," I blurted out.

Jeff laughed. "As a matter of fact, I have. We just finished dissecting a frog at my other school, so I kind of have the jump on all this stuff. Excuse the pun." He scooped up his frog and nodded to his partner. "Let's face Mr. Giandi and get this over with."

When they left, Laura turned to me and grinned. "He's cute!" Then she looked back at the frog and groaned. "We've got thirty more minutes to get this thing in shape."

At the rate we were going, we'd be one of the last teams to show our frog to Mr. Giandi. Everything has to be dissected, labeled, and stuffed back into the frog. That was the tough part. Laura handed me the parts, and I stuck a little marker on them, but somehow there seemed to be more pieces than we started out with.

"What do you think he'll do, exactly?" Laura sounded worried.

"Mr. Giandi? He'll look at the frog and make sure we labeled everything right, and then he'll ask us some questions about the different systems." I flipped open the textbook. "Most of the questions are at the end of the chapter."

"I think we've about got it," Laura said breathlessly. She picked up a piece of something that looked like wet spaghetti and crammed it in the frog. "Small intestines," she said proudly. She planted a flag on it as if she had just discovered Antarctica. "Let's go," she said.

I gingerly picked up the frog and headed for the sink.

"Where are you going?"

"I just want to rinse out the body cavity.

The fumes from the formaldehyde are driving me crazy, and besides, he'll look . . . neater."

"Tracy, for heaven's sake, be careful with him." She hurried over to me. "If anything happens to Kermit, I'll have to kill myself."

"What could happen?" I said glibly. "He'll look better if he's clean, and he won't smell so bad." The next minute, disaster struck. I was holding Kermit over the sink in my left hand, and I gently turned the water on. The trouble was the water didn't come on gently. It blasted out like a tidal wave, and nearly knocked Kermit out of my hand.

"Tracy, grab him!" Laura yelled.

I managed to hang on to Kermit with both hands while she turned off the tap, but it was too late. I was afraid to look, but Laura's moan said it all. Kermit was a shell of his former self. All the neatly labeled parts were gone — literally down the drain.

Without thinking, Laura plunged her hand into the sink. "Why didn't you at least have the brains to plug up the drain?" she said angrily.

"I didn't expect anything like this to happen," I said miserably. "It's all my fault."

She glared at me. "It certainly is!" She picked up what was left of Kermit, and tossed it in the wastebasket. "I'll be right back," she said, marching into Mr. Giandi's office.

"What did he say?" I asked a moment later, when she returned.

She plunked a frozen package down on the counter. "Welcome to Kermit II," she said grimly.

I really did feel guilty about dropping Kermit's vital parts down the sink, but somehow I had the feeling that the whole thing was inevitable. It was almost as if I was under a bad spell that day. First oversleeping, then the rain, the pictures, frog day. . . . Kermit was just the last straw in a string of unlucky events.

Luckily, Laura and I are such good friends that I knew she wouldn't stay mad at me for long. She caught up with me at the lockers, and gave me a sheepish smile.

"Still friends?"

I grinned at her. "Of course. How could we let a mere frog come between us?" I paused. "This has really been a lousy day. Everything has gone wrong."

"You should have checked your horoscope. Maybe it would have told you to stay in bed today," she said lightly.

"Laura, that's a terrific idea. Why didn't I think of it?"

"Hey, I was just kidding."

"Well, I'm not. In fact, from now on, that's exactly what I'm going to do. I don't want any more surprises."

I had one more surprise waiting for me, though. Jeff Nichols. I was crossing the parking lot when he fell into step beside me.

"I think I'm off frog legs for life," he said with a smile.

"Me, too." I told him about Kermit II and he was sympathetic.

"That's lousy luck, Tracy."

"I think so, too," I agreed. "Still, I can see Mr. Giandi's point of view. He can't give us a grade on something that's probably floating miles away by now."

Jeff chuckled. 'You're very philosophical about it. I just couldn't be that laid back if it happened to me."

"Well, easy come, easy go." I suddenly felt a little shy with him. He was really nice-looking, with sandy brown hair and blue eyes that crinkled when he laughed. He turned to me and for a moment I was afraid he had caught me staring.

"Would you like a ride home? Or better yet, why don't we stop for a Coke?"

"Uh, sure!" I blurted out. I couldn't believe it. Was my luck finally changing?

After half an hour with Jeff, I felt like I had known him all my life. We liked the same books, the same movies, and both of us got a kick out of trivia questions.

"How many rows of whiskers does a cat have?" Jeff thought he had me on that one.

"Three," I said smugly. "What's the name of Tonto's horse?" I could tell from Jeff's expression that he knew.

"That's an easy one. Scout."

"I thought I had you stumped." I sighed and finished my drink. Then I got it. "I know," I said triumphantly. "Who was Howdy Doody's brother?"

A pained look crossed his face, and I knew I had him. "It was. . . . It's no use, I can't remember," he said finally. "Okay, who was it?"

"You're not going to believe this, but I can't remember either!"

"That's not fair," Jeff said. He put his arm lightly over my shoulder and we laughed all the way back to the car.

It was one of the best afternoons of my life.

Three

"Well, somebody certainly had a good day. You look like you just won the sweepstakes."

"Who, me?" I said innocently. "Believe it or not, Mom, this started out as one of the worst days of my life."

"Why do I have the sneaking suspicion that it changed for the better?" She grinned and starting cutting up vegetables for stew. Every once in a while, Mom goes on a natural foods kick and decides that everything has to be made from scratch. Luckily, her obsessions don't last long, and Tom and I can usually go back to eating Twinkies the next day.

I poured myself a glass of milk, and sat down next to Tom, who was reading *Computer Finds* from cover to cover. I think that if Tom was ever shipwrecked on a desert island, he'd be happy if he had a few back issues of *Computer Finds* to keep him company.

"The crazy thing is, today really did change for the better. It went from absolutely horrible to fantastic, all in the space of a few minutes." I paused. "What does that sound like to you?"

"It sounds like there's a boy involved in the story somewhere." Sometimes my mother has a really disconcerting way of being right on target.

Tom managed to tear himself away from the magazine. "A boy? Hey, did you and Rick —"

"Please," I interrupted him. "I've got a weak stomach."

"I'm just asking," he said in a hurt voice. "If you got to know Rick, you'd really like him. He's the kind of guy who sort of . . ."

Grows on you, I added silently.

". . . grows on you." He smiled, pleased with himself.

I pictured Rick as a giant, creeping fungus, ready to devour me. Gross! I shook my head quickly to dispel the image. "Want me to help with dinner?" I asked Mom.

"I'm just about finished," she said thoughtfully. "I've added barley and turnips to some beef stock, so it should be good and nourishing. It's real country-style stew."

Tom caught my eye and pretended to gag. "I'd go easy on the barley, Mom." I was surprised he'd spoken up.

"You and Tracy loved this the last time I made it," she said reproachfully.

Correction, Mom. We pretended to love it.

25

It tasted like dog food, and if we hadn't filled up on double cheeseburgers after school, I don't know what we would have done. I left Mom and Tom-Boy in the kitchen arguing over the vitamin content of carrot peels and escaped to my room.

I love my room. Everyone else thinks it's a mess, but I prefer to think of it as "creative disorder." I suppose you'd call the style eclectic. That was one of our vocabulary words this week, and it means a little of this, a little of that. Everything is supposed to blend into a harmonious whole, and I think my room really does. It takes a lot of imagination to mix wicker furniture and a leopard skin rug and make it all work.

I flopped down on my brass bed, and reached after my math book. My hand touched the astrology book instead, just as if it was meant to. *Why argue with fate?* Math can wait, I decided. The "secrets of the stars" were almost within my reach, just pages away! According to the cover, there was no problem too tough for astrology. It could help me make sense out of the crazy things that happened every day . . . bring happiness and romance to my life . . . unravel my friends' personalities . . . make me smarter and richer . . . and it would even cure my migraine headaches!

The last statement was a little puzzling, because I don't even get migraine headaches. But I liked the idea of being smarter and richer. Especially smarter, I thought guiltily, looking at my unopened math book. The promises were endless. With a little patience, I might even learn to predict the future. The stars were ready to teach me.

I could hardly wait to start. And naturally, I decided to start with myself. Pisces. I was just getting into all the exciting facets of my personality — the book insisted that not only was I witty and charming, but I was unbelievably creative — when the phone rang.

"Yes," I barked, annoyed at the interruption.

"Well, don't take my head off!" It was Laura. "The least you can do is be pleasant. You owe me one after Kermit, remember?"

"Sorry," I muttered. "I was right in the middle of something."

"Anything interesting?"

"Quadratic equations," I lied swiftly. I wondered if Pisceans are known for their truthfulness. I'd have to remember to check that, once I got Laura off the phone.

"Well, I've got something crazy to tell you. The most unbelievable thing has just happened to me." I waited. There was a dramatic pause, and then Laura cleared her throat impatiently. "Aren't you dying to ask me what it is?"

I played the game. "What is it?"

"Four Eyes asked me out. Probably because you turned him down. I nearly died!"

"Four Eyes? You mean. . . ."

"That's right. Rick Jacobs. He just called

and asked me out for pizza a week from Friday."

"What did you tell him?"

"That I had a terminal disease and wouldn't be available. And that I also was joining a convent."

"What did you really tell him?"

She groaned. "What difference does it make? I told him that I couldn't go. What do you think!"

"I'm not sure that was a good idea," I said slowly.

"What! Have you lost your mind? I think all that formaldehyde must have pickled your brain, Tracy."

"Look, I can't explain it, but a lot of weird things have happened." I hesitated. "Do you ever get the feeling that there's a reason for everything that happens? That there are forces governing our lives we don't even know about?"

"No."

I suddenly wanted to make her understand. "I read my horoscope the other night. The night that Rick was here."

"And . . . ?" she prompted.

"And it sounds crazy, but it all fit. It said that my math test would be canceled and postponed, and that a friend from third grade would call me."

"It said all that?" she asked incredulously.

"Well, not in so many words, but the meaning was clear. And today was a disaster, except for —" I stopped suddenly. Of course!

28

I had forgotten to check my horoscope that morning. All my problems could have been avoided. Why hadn't I thought of it earlier? "Laura, I've got to hang up and check on something. I'll talk to you later." I could hear her sputtering as I slammed the receiver down. I hated to be rude to my best friend, but some things just won't wait.

"Where is it?" I dashed into the kitchen just as Mom was emerging with the dreaded stew.

"Where's what?"

"Today's paper," I said breathlessly.

"I think Dad's reading it —"

I didn't wait for her to finish — I darted into the living room. "Dad, I need the paper. For a school project."

He peered at me over his glasses. "Hi, Tracy. It's nice to see you."

"Hi, Dad," I said, ignoring the sarcasm. "Now can I have the paper?"

"Which section do you want?"

"The one with the . . . the weather," I improvised quickly. If the horoscope section wasn't there, I'd be out of luck. My luck held. It was there. I grabbed it and found what I wanted.

PISCES. Beware of an important appointment. It's one you can't afford to miss. Negative vibrations dominate the day until late afternoon when signs improve and you'll reconcile with a friend. Don't be led astray by false dreams of romance.

Most of the horoscope fit perfectly. It was

amazing. I had forgotten an important appointment that morning. Actually two appointments, the photographer and Kermit. And the day had gotten a lot better in the afternoon. I thought of Jeff and felt a silly grin spread over my face. Laura, of course, was the friend that I reconciled with. Everything was neat and tidy. Except the last line. *Don't be led astray by false dreams of romance.* Surely that couldn't mean Jeff, I decided. But what did it mean?

I was still puzzling over it when Laura called around nine o'clock. "I thought you'd at least call me back and tell me what was so important." Her voice was frosty.

I decided I better explain what was going on, or our reconciliation would be short-lived. I told her about the astrology book, the way people's signs seemed to fit their personalities, and the horoscope. And I told her about Jeff.

She didn't say much, and I couldn't tell if she was convinced or not. "The horoscope was true," I told her, "right down to the letter."

"What about Jeff, and the false romance? Do you really believe that?"

"Well, that part doesn't quite make sense to me," I said. "Sometimes horoscopes are hard to interpret. It takes a lot of practice."

"If you really like Jeff — and you seem to — it can't be true," she insisted. "It must mean something else. I know! Maybe it means Rick Jacobs."

"Very funny, but I don't think so. You're the one he asked out today, not me."

"Why don't you check my horoscope," she said suddenly. "This will be a good test."

I hunted for the paper and dragged it on the bed. "Okay, here goes. April fifth. You're an Aries."

"I know I am," she said impatiently. "Just read it."

"A friend's carelessness will cause you aggravation . . ."

"Aggravation is right! You dropped Kermit down the sink today. That must be what they're talking about."

". . . and your good looks will win you attention."

"Right again. The school photographer told me I should be a model. . . ."

"Don't turn down a suitor too quickly. Remember that love comes in many disguises." There was a pause while we both tried to figure that one out.

"Well, that part certainly doesn't fit," Laura said finally. "You almost had me going for a minute. But they really goofed that time, because the only 'suitor' I've had today is. . . ."

"Rick Jacobs," I finished for her. We both were silent, stunned by the awful implications. *Loves comes in many disguises. . . .*

Laura recovered first, and managed a nervous giggle. "Tracy, for heaven's sake, don't you see it's all just a joke? I mean, *Rick Jacobs.* Give me a break!"

"You have to admit it's strange," I said softly. "Everything in your horoscope and my horoscope fits. Except that."

"Well, they can't be right about every single little detail. I don't see you worrying about false romance," she said shrewdly. "I bet if Jeff calls you, you'll go out with him in a minute."

I felt ridiculously pleased at the idea, but I didn't want to let on. "Maybe," I said slowly. "But if I do, I'll be careful. Because there's more to this astrology business than meets the eye. I just know it!"

"Pisceans never did have much sense," Laura said with a sigh. "Well, if the stars tell you that Rick Springfield plans on asking me out for lunch tomorrow, let me know, okay? I'll need half an hour to set my hair."

It was really late when I turned the light out, but I couldn't sleep. The astrology book was remarkable. I finished the section on Pisces, and learned a lot of interesting things about myself. There were whole aspects of my personality and talents that I hadn't even used.

For one thing, Pisceans are born poets. It seemed a little odd that I had never had the urge to write poetry before, but I decided then and there to start keeping a notebook with me at all times. I've heard that a lot of famous writers do that, and why should I be any different? When inspiration struck, I wanted to be ready.

I made a note on my memo pad. *Buy note-*

book. I hesitated, and then added, *Check out poetry books from library.* It never hurts to see what other people are doing. But what kind of poetry? The poetry in my English lit book was no help. It was full of bloody battlefields and Grecian urns. Not my style at all.

I turned back to the astrology book. *Pisceans are dreamy romantics, full of mysterious wisdom,* it said. *They need to belong to someone more than they need to eat, sleep, or breathe. Tender, playful, and affectionate, they thrive on love.* The answer was clear. I should be writing love poetry. I decided right then and there to start reading Elizabeth Barrett Browning every day. It gave me a funny, excited feeling to think that someday my poetry would be on the library shelf with hers.

I couldn't get over how much I had learned about myself in such a short space of time. And all because of one book.

The chapter on Pisces could have been written just for me. Of course I already knew that I tend to be sentimental — I cried when Bambi's mother got shot and during lots of other movies — and that I have a tender heart and a forgiving nature. And I also suspected that I was capable of deep, passionate feelings and possessed a keen intelligence.

But to think that I was a natural poet? To think that someday thousands of readers would melt at words I would put on paper. I sighed happily and settled back into the pillows. I wasn't sure, but I thought I felt a poem coming on. Should I reach for the memo pad? No, let it flow, I decided. The moonlight filtered through my drapes and made a pattern on the bedspread. There should be a poem somewhere in that, shouldn't there? I frowned and tried to think, but a bunch of silly rhymes crowded in my head.

Night . . . bright . . . light . . . sight. Nothing seemed to fit. I parted the drapes a little more. The moonlight poured into the room like . . . liquid silver. That wasn't too bad, I decided. But could silver be liquid? I'd have to ask my chemistry teacher tomorrow. And one line certainly wasn't a poem. I had a long way to go if I wanted to fill a book.

I snuggled back under the covers. The closest I had come to writing poetry before was in my high school yearbook. "Roses are red, violets are blue. . . ." I hesitated. "If you can write poetry, I can too."

Not a great beginning. But probably even Mrs. Browning had her off days.

Four

I woke up expecting to have a brilliantly constructed poem in my head. I didn't. I read once that a lot of writers do their most creative work while they're asleep. They have dozens of exciting dreams and their brain leads them down unexplored pathways. All they have to do the next day is put everything down on paper.

Unfortunately, I'm not one of them.

I felt like my brain was stuffed with Kleenex when Mom bombarded me awake. "This is the second time this week you've overslept, Tracy! You must be staying up too late. If you don't shape up, I'm going to have to give you a curfew like an eight-year-old!"

I let the shower run on me for a long time. I stepped out very pink and wrinkled, but at least I could focus my eyes.

Mom had made a strange concoction for breakfast. It was some kind of health drink that had a whole day's supply of vitamins and nutrients. I didn't see why you needed a whole day's supply. I suppose it would be handy if you were trekking to Siberia, or the Amazon jungle, but Tom and I would be having lunch in just three and a half hours.

I stared at Tom. He was reading a computer magazine at the table, and he was in a world of his own. Mom doesn't mind if we read at breakfast, because we don't usually sit down at the same time anyway. Dad leaves for work very early, before any of us are even up.

The health drink smelled horrible. I flipped open my math book and tried to lose myself in quadratic equations. Just to show you how totally different we are, Tom used to do equations for *fun* when he was my age. He'd curl up in Dad's big leather chair with a pile of paper, and while away the day solving for x. He liked the really tough problems the best. The ones that took two or three sheets of paper. It was enough to make you gag.

"Are you having a test today?" Mom asked. It was more of an accusation than a question, and I was immediately on my guard. Parents are very good at that. They don't always ask questions because they want to know the answer. Sometimes they already *do* know the answer, and they want to see you squirm a little.

"Just a quiz," I said as casually as I could.

She stared at me, and I could tell she wasn't completely taken in. "You haven't been studying much lately, Tracy. You're not spending too much time on this new hobby of yours, are you?"

"Hobby?"

"I've seen that astrology book," she said. "You lug it everywhere you go. I'd hate to think you were neglecting your studies to become a . . . fortune-teller."

I laughed. "Mom, believe me, I'm not going to be a dropout, or a fortune-teller. Anyway, I'm learning quite a bit about myself lately. Things that will be very helpful later on."

"What sort of things?" She looked a little suspicious, and I decided to downplay the whole thing.

"Oh, just things about my personality. Like my talents, my strong points. And I'm learning about the rest of the family, too." I nodded to Tom, who still had his nose buried in the computer book. "Tom is very cool and analytical, which is what you'd expect from an Aquarian, and since I'm a Piscean, I'm passionate and creative."

I thought I caught Mom smiling, and I said defensively, "Well, that's what the book said."

"Do you really think you can sum up Tom so easily? Don't you think there's any depth to his personality? Any quirks or surprises?"

Frankly, I didn't, but I figured it wasn't the most tactful thing in the world to say. "Mom, you have to admit, he's pretty predictable." I lowered my voice, but I needn't have bothered. Tom was hopelessly wrapped up in the world of bits and bytes. "He's the typical absent-minded scientist."

We both turned to watch Tom. His eyes were focused on the page, but one hand jutted out for the health drink. His movements were stiff and mechanical, like a robot's.

I watched, horrified, as he brought the foamy green mixture to his lips. No one in their right mind would drink it. The smell alone would stop them cold. No one except Tom. Without looking up, he drained the glass and set it back on the table. Maybe he felt our eyes on him, because he blinked foggily at us, like he was coming out of a trance.

"You drank it!" I whispered. "I can't believe it." I also couldn't believe that he was still alive, but I didn't want to hurt Mom's feelings.

He looked at the empty glass like he had never seen it before. "Oh, this?" he said absently. "Sure, it was great." There was a pause. "What was it?" He looked at Mom, then at me.

I picked up my books and stood up. "I rest my case," I said softly.

"I beat you to it." Laura caught me between classes and shoved a newspaper clipping in my face. It was the daily horoscope.

"I thought you didn't believe in those things," I teased her.

"I don't. At least, not completely. But, you

never know, do you? I thought it wouldn't hurt to check."

I scanned the paper. "A day when completely unexpected and dramatic events could occur. . . ."

"Do you have anything special planned for today?"

"Nothing." When I read the next line, I felt a funny little tingle go down my spine. "A meeting with a friend can bring happy results, but don't confuse love and friendship."

Laura peered at me. "That's the second time it's warned you about that," she said thoughtfully.

"Well, I think they're wrong on both counts today. Nothing exciting has happened, and —"

"Don't look now, but your friend just showed up."

"What? Laura, are you talking about —"

"Hi, Tracy." I whirled around to face Jeff Nichols' deep blue eyes. "What are you up to?"

"Hi, Jeff," I said, finding my voice. "Laura and I were just. . . ." I turned to include Laura in the conversation, but she was gone. "Just talking," I said, feeling a little foolish.

"Tracy, I just wanted you to know that if you need any help on Kermit II, I'm available," he offered.

"Thanks, but I think we've got it straightened out. Mr. Giandi is going to let us into the lab during lunch hour to work on him.

It was nice of you to think of it, though."

He shrugged and smiled at me. "What are friends for?"

Friends! Just like the column predicted. Well, what did I expect? Jeff was just being polite. He was cute, and smart, and a lot of fun to be with. But that was hardly the start of a wild love affair. I had no intention of confusing friendship with love.

"I had a great time the other day," he said, still looking at me with those unbelievable eyes.

That shook me up a little, but I was determined not to show it. *He's just being friendly,* I reminded myself for the dozenth time. It would have been easier to remember if he had looked like Rick Jacobs.

"I thought you might like to grab a hamburger for lunch today. They're serving creamed chipped beef in the cafeteria," he added, as if he thought I needed some extra persuasion.

"I'd love it." I couldn't get over how cool I was acting. My voice was steady, but my mind was racing.

Completely unexpected and dramatic events. . . . I could hardly wait to tell Laura.

"Everybody knows the name of the newspaper Superman worked for," Jeff began as soon as we ordered.

"The Daily Planet." I pretended to yawn from boredom.

"But not everyone knows the name of the editor," he pointed out.

"Perry White."

"Okay, so you're very unusual." He laughed, showing a set of white, even teeth. He looked really attractive in a light blue sweater that showed off his broad shoulders. I caught myself wondering why he had asked me out to lunch. There were dozens of great-looking girls who would love to go out with him.

In fact, a whole table of cheerleaders had been giving him the eye ever since we sat down. It he noticed, he never let on, even when one of them managed to spill half a cup of ice on him. "Sorry!" she said breathlessly. "My tray kind of overbalanced." She flashed a toothpaste smile at him, and waited.

"Accidents happen," he said mildly, and went right on talking to me. "Let's see, where were we?"

"You were trying to stump me on a trivia question, and you weren't having any luck. Maybe you're out of your league," I told him.

"We'll see who's out of whose league." He took a giant bite of cheeseburger and closed his eyes. "Okay, I've got it. What movie won the award for the worst vegetable horror film ever made?"

I pretended to be lost in thought, but I knew the answer right away. *The Attack of the Killer Tomatoes.*

"I can't believe it!"

"It happens to be one of my favorite movies," I said modestly.

"Mine, too." He looked at me in astonishment. "You know, this whole thing is so incredible. I don't think I've ever met anyone that I had so much in common with." He paused and shook his head. "You're the only girl I know who's even heard of that film. In fact, if I told you my second favorite movie, you'd probably burst out laughing."

"No, I wouldn't," I said softly.

"It's —"

I reached over and gently put my finger over his lips. *The Invasion of the Mushroom People.* I smiled at him. "You see, it's mine, too."

If I had had a camera, I would have loved to have caught the expression on his face.

"Where were you!" Laura demanded, as we filed into P.E. "There were supposed to be three of us for lunch, remember? You, me, and Kermit II."

"Oh, no."

"Oh, yes. I covered for you with Mr. Giandi. I said you were buying a sandwich and would be there in a minute. Anyway, it was creepy being in that lab alone with just a frog for company. Have you ever looked at some of the specimens they have in there? Do you know, they even have a whole jar of —"

"Laura," I interrupted quickly. "I'm really sorry about not going to the lab. Jeff Nichols asked me out for lunch, and I completely forgot."

"Oh. Well, that's different," she said, mollified. "I'd pick Jeff Nichols over Kermit any day. In fact, I'd almost pick Rick Jacobs over Kermit, but I'm not sure."

"At least Kermit doesn't wear Hawaiian shirts," I giggled. "And I'll go straight to the lab after school and do my share of the work, okay?"

"If you insist." Laura did a little pirouette in front of the locker room mirror. We were wearing identical basketball uniforms of heavy blue cotton. She looked like she'd stepped out of a sportswear ad. I looked like I had slept in my clothes.

"Laura, has anything strange happened lately?"

"Strange?" She tied her hair back with a matching blue ribbon.

"Unusual. Out of the ordinary."

"Not really. I didn't even bother reading my horoscope today, if that's what you're getting at."

"I still have it." I reached for my notebook. "Don't say no to a dazzling stranger. Exercise caution at work and play. Better safe than sorry."

"That's weird." Laura was finally satisfied with her appearance and headed for the door. "Let's go, Tracy," she said over her shoulder. Unfortunately, Helen Roberts came barreling in the door at that exact moment. I don't know much about reincarnation, but if Helen ever comes back to earth, she'll probably be a Pittsburgh Pirate. She's tall, weighs about one-sixty, and collects pictures of discus throwers.

She's about as delicate as a Mack truck, and she literally bowled Laura over. "Laura!" I squealed, and ran to help her. Together, Helen and I got Laura back on her feet. Or at least, back on one foot.

"Ooh, my ankle," she cried. "I think it's broken." She was jumping around like a demented flamingo when Mrs. Masters, the gym teacher, came in to see what all the commotion was about.

"Everybody out," she said firmly. "Tracy, get a bucket of ice. Laura, stop moving so much. You'll only make it worse."

The ice didn't help much, and Laura's ankle tripled in size. It was fascinating to watch, in a grotesque sort of way.

"It's puffing up just like a loaf of bread in the oven," Helen chortled. "I remember, I sprained my ankle once —" Laura stopped her with a look. She's very good at that. She gives these icy stares that only green-eyed people can manage.

"Do you think it's sprained, Mrs. Masters?"

She looked at the ballooning ankle and frowned. "It could be, I suppose. Anyway, it certainly needs x-rays. I'm going to call your mother, Laura." In spite of Mrs. Masters' order, the girls were crowding around Laura. "I hope this is a lesson to everybody,"

Mrs. Masters snapped. "Don't come bursting in that swinging door so carelessly. Use a little common sense, a little caution, so you don't hit someone on the other side. I've told you that a hundred times." She sighed and headed for the phone. "You know what they say. . . ."

Her voice trailed off. I looked up to see Laura's eyes boring holes into me. We were both thinking of the same thing. *Better safe than sorry.*

"Rhett Butler's horse in *Gone With the Wind*," a familiar voice hissed in my ear.

"He didn't have a horse." Jeff groaned and fell into step beside me. "I bet you don't know how many years the Starship Enterprise was supposed to be in space."

"Five. It was my favorite show. And I suppose you know Spock was a —"

"Vulcan."

He laughed. "I think we're evenly matched. How about a Coke to celebrate?"

"Celebrate what?"

"Star Trek, the fact that it's Friday, our friendship. Whatever."

"I'd like to, but I have a date with a frog." I explained about Kermit II.

"You can't go into the lab alone. Didn't you ever see *The Brain That Wouldn't Die?*"

"You've got me on that one."

"It's about a beautiful young girl who goes into a lab alone. I'll skip the gory details, but she ends up as a pickled brain. I can't let that happen to you," he said, pushing open the door to the biology lab. "I'll never find another girl who knows the name of Frankenstein's granddaughter."

I dumped my books on the counter, and faced him. "Maria."

"You see?" He moved a little closer, and for one crazy moment, I thought he was going to kiss me. "We have so much in common, we could be twins."

"Or best friends," I blurted out. I don't know what made me say it, except that the line from the horoscope came back to haunt me. *Don't confuse love and friendship.* It would be tough, being around a terrific guy like Jeff, but I was determined to protect myself.

A funny expression flickered in Jeff's eyes. Surprise? Disappointment? I couldn't be sure. Then he smiled and said very casually, "Sure. Best friends. That's exactly what we'll be." He reached for a dissecting kit. "Let's see what we can do with Kermit II."

F*ive*

"He did it again!" Laura's voice was about three octaves higher than usual, so I knew something momentous had happened. Aries are very excitable — I learned that from the astrology book — and you have to be patient with them. I took a deep breath and waited.

"Who did what again?" I said in my calmest voice.

"Rick Jacobs. He asked me out again. Can you believe it?" She paused to polish off a giant bowl of ice cream. "There's more in the kitchen if you want some," she offered. "Coffee, chocolate, and butter pecan. Mom bought gallons of ice cream and gingerale on the way home from the doctor's."

"She must think you had your tonsils out. Before you start on Rick Jacobs, how's your ankle?" Laura was stretched out on the sofa in a quilted robe, every inch the invalid.

"Oh, it's nothing. I mean, it still *hurts*,"

she added quickly when she caught my look, "but nothing's broken. It was just a sprain, they said. No thanks to Helen the Hindenberg."

I laughed. "I see you haven't lost your sense of humor."

"It's a good thing I haven't, with all the crazy things that have been happening," she said darkly. "And Rick Jacobs is the craziest of all. He called me a few minutes ago and asked me out again."

"What did you tell him?"

"Well, luckily, I had the perfect excuse." She grinned. "It was almost worth it to sprain my ankle. He's quicker than I thought, though. He actually suggested that we spend the evening here, watching TV."

"Just the two of you on the sofa. How romantic." I paused. "So you said no to a dazzling stranger. . . . I wonder if that was such a good idea," I said softly.

"What?"

"The horoscope. Don't you remember? It warned you to be careful, and it also warned you not to say no to a dazzling stranger."

"Rick Jacobs, a dazzling stranger? Don't make me laugh. The only thing dazzling about him is his fillings. Since you brought up the subject, you don't happen to have that astrology book with you, do you?"

"Sure. Do you want to check something?"

"I want to see what it says about Aries." I handed her the book, and she flipped through it. "I already know quite a bit about my sign, of course. Aries people tend to be warm, sensitive, and extremely intelligent."

I tried not to smile. Maybe Laura didn't realize it, but the book said wildly flattering things about people born under every sign. Of course, maybe that was just good psychology. I know I'd be discouraged if I read that Pisceans were slow, stupid, and lazy.

"Ha! Just as I thought." Laura propped herself up on the sofa pillows and started to read aloud. "Listen to what it says about me, Tracy. I'm romantic, dramatic, and daring."

"That must be why Rick Jacobs finds you so irrestible," I said under my breath.

"I'm like a light in the forest, or a firecracker on the Fourth of July. I'm bright, ambitious, loyal, and utterly faithful in matters of love."

"Good. I'm sure Rick will be glad to hear that." She heard me that time and frowned.

"Honestly, Tracy, I thought you took this seriously. I'm trying to discover new truths about myself, and you make cracks."

"I'm sorry. I guess I've got a lot on my mind. It's been sort of a crazy day for me, too."

Laura was instantly apologetic. "Hey, I'm sorry. Here I've been rambling on about myself, and I didn't even ask you what you've been doing."

I almost told her that that was a typical Aries trait, but I decided against it. After all, she's sick, I reminded myself. "I saw Jeff after school. He helped me with Kermit II.

In fact, he did such a good job on the dissecting, Mr. Giandi might get suspicious."

"You can always drop him down the sink again," Laura said. "Just to shake things up a little." She took a swig of gingerale and looked at me. "So, it's a hot romance with you and Jeff?"

"No," I said quickly, "nothing like that. We're just friends."

"Sure. . . ." she drawled. She gave me a mischievous smile. "Where have I heard that before? What's wrong? Isn't he the right sign?"

I had to laugh. "I haven't even checked on that. No, it's just that . . . well, it's the way things are." I thought of the horoscope. *Don't confuse friendship with love.* "It's the way he wants things, too."

"I don't believe that for a minute," she said firmly. "I bet you're perfect for each other, and don't even know it. Would you feel better if the horoscope said so?"

I shook my head, but I didn't fool her.

"What's his sign?"

"I've got no idea. We never even talked about anything like that."

"It doesn't matter. We can find out in a jiffy." She dragged the phone onto her lap. "I don't suppose he's in the phone book yet, but we can get the number from information."

"Laura, what are you doing?"

She was already talking to the operator

and jotting down a number. "Just be quiet," she said, dialing quickly.

I was too stunned to ask any more questions. Laura is always doing crazy, impulsive things, and this obviously was one of them.

"Hello, Mrs. Nichols?" She was holding her nose and doing a fairly good impression of the school secretary. "This is Miss Grimes at the high school. I'm just checking some facts for our computer, and I wondered if you could give me Jeffrey's date of birth? . . . October twenty-first. Thank you very much." She hung up and giggled. "I think that makes him a Libra. You better watch out." She handed me back the astrology book. "You should keep this. You're going to need it more than I do."

"Are Libras that dangerous?"

She nodded very seriously. "I'm afraid so. They're incredibly magnetic, and you want to be around them forever." She laughed. "Unfortunately, they never stick around for long. Bernie Hildebrande was a Libra."

"Who's Bernie Hildebrande?"

She sighed and hugged the pillow. "He was someone I met at camp three summers ago. Tall and blond, and he even had hair on his chest — well, he had hair on his chest if the light was right —"

It took Laura forever to tell a story. "Laura just give me the bottom line," I pleaded.

"I'm getting to it," she said indignantly. "Well, Bernie and I fell madly in love. We took long walks in the rain, and carved our initials on the Camp Minnetauket rowboat. I was crazy over him, and he said he'd love me forever."

"And . . . ?"

She shrugged. "We went steady for a day and a half. I never saw him again."

"Oh." I was beginning to wish I had never heard about Bernie Hildebrande.

"That's just the way Librans are, Tracy." She smiled at me. "They're fun and exciting, and they absolutely ruin you for other guys." She paused. "But as long as you don't get romantically involved with one. . . ."

"They make great friends."

"Exactly."

I should have been thrilled at the news, but somehow it was tough to manage a smile.

It was amazing, but the more I got into astrology, the more everything seemed to fit. People's personalities just seemed to fall into place and I could read them like a book.

Tom and Dad were easy. They were Aquarians, through and through. They were cool, logical, and very scientific in their approach to things. They both loved computers and puzzles, and were so compulsive they never left the cap off the toothpaste.

They used reason to solve their problems, and never relied on sheer instinct, like I did. We were complete opposites. I was very intuitive, practically psychic, and trusted my feelings. My heart ruled my head, which made me a complete mystery to them.

Laura was an Aries, and that made sense, too. She's very bright, and entertaining, but she tends to look at things from her own point of view. She's involved in a million projects at once, and sometimes, it's exhausting just to be around her.

And then there was Jeff.

The moment I got home from Laura's house, I curled up in the window seat and read the whole chapter on Libra. My worst fears were realized. Librans were very attractive to women, but they were also known to be very fickle. According to the book, they were the ultimate playboys of the universe. In other words, they were marvelous to be around, but terrible to fall in love with.

Laura was right. Jeff was dangerous. Or at least he could be, if I let myself get involved with him. The book was very clear on that. "Once you're caught and enmeshed in the Libran charm, it won't be easy to break away. When he smiles at you, something will happen inside. Your heart will turn over."

It was all true. There *was* something special about that smile! I had been right to steel myself against it. It's a good thing I had my instincts going for me, or I might have been swept away. "He'll use every trick with casual ease, and seldom fail to get the girl. However, once he gets her, he's off in hot pursuit of another pretty face. . . ."

Not only were Librans charming, they were impossibly cruel! I was better off without him. I finished the rest of the chapter quickly, and the news didn't get any better. "Librans care far more about themselves than for anyone they could meet. A serious relationsip is impossible with these delightful dreamers. If you fall in love with one, be forewarned. Or run the other way."

I closed the book and stared out the window. I had learned more about Libras than I ever wanted to. I thought about Jeff. It was crazy, but he didn't seem like a Libra. Of course, he was very attractive and was terrific to be around. That part was certainly true. But as far as being selfish . . . uncaring . . . fickle? None of that seemed to fit. He had been really nice that day in the lab, dissectink Kermit II. And when he took me out to lunch, he ignored Debbie Watson who practically threw herself at him.

According to the book, none of those things should have happened. I stretched and stood up. Maybe I was just trying to rearrange things the way I wanted them. I knew deep down that I liked Jeff a lot, but I also knew that anything romantic was out of the question.

"Jeff and I are just friends," I said aloud. I repeated it two more times, like a magic incantation. Maybe saying it would make it so. Now if I could just make myself believe it!

I sat in my room after dinner, feeling

lonely and more than a little sorry for myself. (According to the book, that's one of the few unfavorable traits that I have.) It was a rainy Friday night, and I felt like doing . . . what? I didn't even know. I just knew that I felt bored and at loose ends.

I picked up the astrology book, and then put it down. I couldn't get over how much I had learned from it in the space of a few days. Of course, the news was mixed. On one hand, I discovered that Jeff, who seemed to be a really neat guy, was destined to be my friend, and no more. If only he wasn't a Libran! *The ultimate playboys of the universe.*

But on the other hand, I discovered that Pisceans have a real talent for writing. A talent that I hadn't even bothered developing, I thought guiltily, as I looked at the blank notebook. Earlier in the week, I had checked out a bunch of poetry books from the library, and they were still sitting unread on my nighttable. Somehow, I hadn't had the chance to open them. I picked up the Browning book and started thumbing through it.

I didn't know too much about Elizabeth Barrett Browning, except that she lived in the 1800's and wrote terribly romantic poems to her husband. He was a poet, too, according to the flyleaf. But even more remarkable was the fact that he actually rescued her from her father's house on Wimpole Street! This was a little hard to believe, as she was forty years old at the time, and you'd think she could have left home whenever she wanted. Anyway, they eloped and went to Italy and spent all day writing passionate things to each other.

It didn't seem like a bad life, and I caught myself wondering if she was a Pisces, like me. I really liked her poetry, because it was simple, but it said a lot. "How do I love thee? Let me count the ways. . . ." And then she does! I like poems that do what they say they're going to do.

Mrs. Browning was obviously crazy about her husband, and didn't care if the whole world knew it. The trouble was, it was impossible for me to read her love poetry without thinking of Jeff. I steeled myself against remembering his smile, his laugh, and the way his arm felt when it curled around me.

And the crazy trivia questions. They kept popping into my head at odd hours of the day and night. Without meaning to, I'd try to remember some, so I could stump Jeff with them — just so I could see that grin of his. I caught myself daydreaming about being with him, when I should have been trying to forget him.

I was wondering how to begin writing a poem, when Mom came in with a piece of chocolate cake. "You skipped dessert," she said, with a grin. "Sure you're not sick?"

"I'm not sick. I just had some thinking to do, and I wanted to be by myself for awhile."

She peered at me. "Are you sure you're okay, Tracy?" She sat down on the bed next to me. "You've been acting kind of strange lately. And you're spending a lot of time alone. What's Laura up to tonight, anyway?"

I explained about Laura's ankle, but I left out the part about the horoscope.

"So you're feeling a little down, with your best friend out of commission," she said sympathetically.

"Something like that."

"Well, cheer up. You know what they say. Things have a way of looking up when you least expect them to."

My mother, the optimist. *A typical Gemini*, I thought, and smiled.

"What's so funny?"

"Oh, just things." I reached for the cake and stopped. "Mom, do you think that there's a right person for everyone in the world?"

"A right person?" She frowned, and then looked at the poetry book. "Like the love of your life, you mean? Gosh, I don't know." She laughed. "It's a nice idea, isn't it? I guess when I was young, I thought so. I had a really romantic view of everthing, and I thought that if you just met the right person, everything would fall into place. Unfortunately, the real world doesn't work like that."

"I know it doesn't," I said sadly.

"Why do I have the feeling this has something to do with a boy? Have you met someone you really like, and there's some sort of problem?"

There was a problem all right, I thought wryly. A cosmic problem! "Mom," I said, "what would you do if you met somebody terrific and charming, and then you found out he was a real playboy? You know, that he just dated girls for a little while and then dumped them and started all over with someone else?"

"This is just a hypothetical question, right?"

"Oh, completely hypothetical," I said innocently. "It's for a story I'm writing." It wasn't really a white lie. Maybe if I talked enough about being a writer, I'd eventually get around to doing it.

She sighed. "And you're sure that this hypothetical boy is what you say he is — the love 'em and leave 'em type? There's no mistake?"

"There's no mistake," I said firmly. The stars were never wrong, I added silently. "He's fantastic, but he's a playboy."

"Well, I hate to say it, but I wouldn't get involved with him, Tracy."

"I see." She was absolutely right, but I hated to hear it. "No matter how terrific he is?"

"No matter how terrific. After all, how long could it last? All those other girls must have thought he was pretty terrific too." She smiled and got a far-away look in her eyes. "It's funny, but I knew somebody exactly like that in college. He was dating my roommate, and she was wild over him. His name was

Michael, and he was . . . fabulous. Tall and handsome, and just so terrific to be around. Really one in a million. But such a playboy!" She laughed. "He even tried to date me."

"What happened?"

"My roommate was out of town over spring break, and I was staying in the dorm. I guess he figured it was the perfect opportunity, and no one would ever know."

"Did you go out with him?"

She shook her head. "No. I was tempted, but . . . no, I didn't go out with him. I decided to play it safe. It's funny. I still remember him after all these years."

"Mom, this is going to sound really crazy, but this Michael . . . do you have any idea when his birthday is?"

"Tracy, it was over twenty years ago." She paused, and then said slowly, "The strange thing is, I do know when his birthday is. It happened to fall on a football weekend, and my roommate made him a big cake. It was the end of September. The thirtieth, I think. Why?"

"Just an idea I'm working on." September thirtieth. Another Libra. It all fit.

Six

Things have a way of looking up when you least expect them to. Maybe Mom had some psychic powers herself, because I got a surprise phone call late Friday night. I thought it would be Laura, but instead I was surprised by a deep male voice. It wasn't Jeff, but someone else who sounded very exciting. "Hello, Tracy? I can't believe I caught you at home." There was a pause, and then a low chuckle. "I guess I should introduce myself. I'm Steve Richards."

"Do I know you?"

"Not yet." Again, the chuckle. "But I know who you are. Peanut butter and dates on cracked wheat. I've seen you in the cafeteria line," he explained. "You probably never noticed me, but I always order a banana sandwich. It drives the cooks right up the wall."

"Why would anyone eat banana sandwiches?" It was a crazy conversation, but I was intrigued.

"The coach says I need more potassium, and bananas are a quick way to get it."

Suddenly a bell went off in my brain. The coach. . . . Football! Steve Richards, star quarterback. I couldn't believe it. "Are you —I mean, is this the Steve Richards who plays football?" I managed to stutter.

"Guilty as charged. Don't hold that last game with the Eagles against me, though. I wasn't up to par."

"You were great," I said sincerely. "My brother's a big fan of yours." It was true. Football was about the only thing that could tear Tom away from the computer screen.

"I'd rather have you as a fan."

"Why?" I said flatly. I'm absolutely no good at flirting, at playing all the cute little games that girls are supposed to know. Laura would have had some witty comeback, but I couldn't think of a line to save my life.

He laughed. "Hey, you're very direct, aren't you? That's okay. I like a girl who doesn't waste time. Okay, you want a straight answer, you'll get one. I think you're cute. Really cute. I've seen you at school a lot, and you're usually alone, or with a girl friend, so I figured you probably weren't going steady with anyone."

Going steady! I've had eight dates in my entire life, and my brother came along on two of them.

"I'm not going steady," I said quietly.

"Great! How about if we go out for pizza tomorrow night? I'll pick you up at seven."

He was pretty direct himself, I thought. He never really asked me to go out, he just assumed I would. I hesitated. What if he was a real animal? I really didn't want to go out with him, but maybe it would take my mind off Jeff. And since Laura was still "laid up," as she said, with her ankle, I'd be spending Saturday night alone in my room. Trying to write poetry. I'd rather tackle Godzilla than struggle with iambic pentameter.

"I'd love to go," I said swiftly.

"We're having granola this morning," Tom said with mock cheerfulness. It wasn't one of Mom's more successful recipes. She makes it the all-natural way, which means it tastes like recycled sawdust.

"I added raisins and dates to it this time, Tracy," she said. "And loads of bran." Tom looked at me and rolled his eyes. Mom thinks that half the world's problems could be solved if people just had enough fiber in their diet. "And wait till you see what we're having for dinner. Mock meatloaf."

"Made entirely of wheat germ," Tom said.

"I won't be here for dinner tonight," I said quickly. "I've got a date." *Mock meatloaf!* Steve was looking better to me all the time.

"That's nice, dear. Anyone we know?"

I shook my head. "No, he's a football player, Steve Richards."

"Hey, way to go!" Tom said suddenly. He stared at me with a mixture of awe and respect. "You should see some of the moves he had in the last game. It was the third quarter, and the ball was on the five yard line. . . ."

Tom's instant replay was interrupted by the phone. "It's for you," Mom said. I could tell from the way she lowered her voice that it was a boy.

"I'll take it in the dining room," I said, dragging the cord behind me. "It's quieter."

I closed the door softly and put on my best phone voice. "Hello."

"Sergeant Friday's badge number on the old Dragnet series."

I smiled to myself. "Seven-fourteen."

"The real name of The Shadow."

"Lamont Cranston."

"The name of Dagwood's dog."

"Daisy." I sighed. "Jeff, those are too easy. When are you going to hit me with the tough ones?"

"I suppose you know who Spiderman really is?"

"Of course. Peter Parker."

There was a loud groan. "I stayed awake half the night thinking of that one."

"You shouldn't have wasted your time. Why don't you just admit that you're licked?"

"Never! You've been lucky, that's all." There was a pause, and then Jeff said, "Just to prove I'm not a sore loser, I'll take you to lunch."

"Okay, that sounds great," I agreed. I felt

like jumping up and down, but I forced myself to be calm. *It's not a real date. It's just a
couple of friends getting together.*

"Where would you like to go?" he asked.

"I'll leave it up to you."

"That's very trusting of you." He laughed.
"You might be in for a surprise."

"I'll take my chances."

"Okay, then. I'll see you at twelve. And
don't get dressed up."

I practically skipped back to the kitchen
and hung up the phone. Mom and Tom were
giving me strange looks. "I'm going out for
lunch," I said, as casually as I could.

"With Steve?" Mom asked.

"No, with Jeff Nichols."

"You mean the 'we're-just-friends' Jeff?"

I could feel a silly grin spreading over my
face. "Uh, right. And we really are just
friends," I added.

Tom snickered and stood up. "Here's the
paper," he said. "You better read Dear Abby
to keep up with your love life."

"Very funny." I grabbed the paper, and
turned to the horoscope section. The words
seemed to jump right off the page at me.
"You've been waiting for a sign, and today
is the day."

Waiting for a sign. Did it mean that I'd
get a sign from Jeff? Was the invitation to
lunch a sign? But what did it mean? Was it
possible we could be more than friends? I
skimmed rapidly over the rest of the horoscope. "Be cheerful, enthusiastic. . . ." I ig-

nored that part. "Spend time with a sick friend." That part was easy. Laura. But the "sign" was the real puzzler.

"I knew you'd like flying kites," Jeff said confidently.

"You've got me all figured out, don't you? No surprises, no mystery to me at all."

"I wouldn't say that. I'm never completely sure what you're going to do next." He tossed a rock into the waves and looked at me. "I'm glad I was right about the kites, though."

"You were. I haven't done this since I was a little kid. And you even picked the perfect day for it." It was very sunny, with a gusty wind that kept the kites dancing in the sky. It was too cold to go swimming, and we had the beach to ourselves.

Jeff and I walked along the edge of the water for a while, and then we decided to stop and have lunch. We tied the kites to a rock, found a sheltered spot behind a sand dune, and spread a blanket. Jeff unpacked some sandwiches and handed me one.

I opened it and did a double take. "I don't believe it," I said. "How did you know?"

"Just a lucky guess."

"C'mon," I teased him. "There can't be that many girls in the world who eat peanut butter and date sandwiches."

"Maybe not," he said, passing me a root beer. "But I knew you were one of them."

I leaned back on a piece of driftwood next to him, and we both stared out at the water.

It was so peaceful being with him. I felt like I had known him forever.

"I'm glad we could see each other today," he said after a minute.

"So am I. And thanks for the kite. How did you know I always wanted a Chinese dragon one?"

"I told you. I know most of your secrets. Maybe I'm a little psychic, just like you." He grinned and put his arm around me.

You can't be. You're a Libra, not a Pisces. I nearly said it aloud, but caught myself just in time. "Do you ever think you are psychic?" I said suddenly. "I mean, do you ever get an idea that something's going to happen before it does?"

He frowned and thought. "Like a premonition, or something?" I nodded. "Sometimes, I guess. But you know, most of that stuff is coincidence, Tracy."

"It is?" *If he knew about the horoscopes, he wouldn't say that! It had been right every time.*

"Sure. There's always a rational explanation for everything, if you dig deep enough." I stared at him. He sounded just like Tom.

"So you don't believe in . . . astrology, or horoscopes, or anything like that," I said slowly.

"Of course not." He laughed, and then said seriously, "Do you?"

"I keep an open mind," I said a little defensively. "There could be some truth to it, you know. A lot of famous people have believed in it."

"'There are more things in heaven and earth than are dreamt of in your philosophy.'" He smiled at me. "Recognize the quotation?"

"That's from Shakespeare," I said automatically. "Hamlet said it to Horatio."

He groaned. "How come I can never get you on anything?"

I laughed and stood up. "You should never tangle with a Pisces."

"A Pisces. That's supposed to mean something, I guess."

"It certainly does. It means I'm bright, intelligent and remarkably talented. I'm sensitive, creative, and have a way with words. So you see, you really don't have a chance."

He put his hands on my shoulders and looked directly in my eyes. "You know something else?" he said.

Was he going to kiss me? I wondered. I was afraid to breathe.

"No, what?" I managed to say.

"You're also very cute." And then he did a funny thing. He leaned over and kissed me on the nose. Then he laughed, grabbed my hand and raced down to the edge of the water.

It was obvious that we were meant to be just friends.

"I don't understand why he didn't ask you out for tonight, if you two had such a terrific time." Laura was eating another gigantic bowl of ice cream and a half-eaten package of Lorna Doones was on the sofa beside her. She was obviously trying to keep up her strength.

"I told you. When it got to be late afternoon, I told Jeff I had to go home to get ready to go out."

"You told him that! What a way to lose a guy."

"I didn't tell him I had another date."

"You didn't have to," she said. "It's not very flattering to be walking hand in hand with someone, and then find out they have to dash home to meet someone else." She paused. "I don't know what your rush was all about anyway. You had plenty of time to get ready for Steve."

"Well, I have to wash my hair, and I wanted to stop by and see you first."

"Oh," she said, in a softer tone. "That was really nice of you, Tracy."

"What are friends for?" I said lightly. I didn't dare tell Laura that it wasn't a matter of choice. I *had* to "spend time with a sick friend," according to the horoscope.

"Horoscopes can be pretty scary, can't they?" For one crazy moment, I thought she was reading my mind.

"What do you mean?"

"Well," she said, munching on a cookie, "since I've hurt my ankle, I've been kind of checking my horoscope every day. Not that I believe in any of it," she added quickly, "but there have been some funny coincidences."

"Jeff says the whole thing is just coincidence," I said suddenly.

"What do you mean?"

"Jeff doesn't believe in astrology," I explained. "We talked a little about it today. I don't even think he knows what sign he is, and he certainly doesn't know anything about Pisces." I waited for her to go on. "You said something about scary. . . ." I prompted her.

"Yeah." She nodded. "The dazzling stranger keeps cropping up."

"Rick Jacobs?"

"In person and on paper. He writes, he calls, he even sent me flowers last week."

"He's in love." I laughed, and then stopped. Poor Rick. I almost felt sorry for him.

"And the crazy thing is that the horoscope predicts it every single time. I never should have started reading those things. It's like a curse. How could Fate be trying to throw us together?"

"I guess even the stars can get mixed up now and then."

"I even checked on his sign," she said. "He's a Capricorn."

"A Capricorn?" I hesitated. Laura was an Aries. "Does that mean what I think it does?"

She nodded miserably. "We're perfect for each other."

Laura and Rick Jacobs destined to be together? Surely it was a giant mistake. A cosmic mistake.

$\mathcal{S}$even

There was absolutely nothing wrong with Steve Richards. He was tall, good-looking, and had the kind of manners that parents love. He sat in the den, talked football with Dad and Tom, and jumped to his feet every time my mother walked into the room. He even polished off a piece of Mom's wheat germ torte with no ill effects. In fact, he would have had a second piece, but I reminded him that we were going out for pizza. He had either the best manners in the world or a cast iron stomach.

"What do you think of Adam's coaching?" Dad asked. "It looked like the guys were confused at the last game. He seemed to change his strategy right after the half." Tom was leaning forward, drinking in every word.

"Yeah, there were some mixed signals," Steve said. "I guess you remember what happened to Rogers in the third quarter?" He said it very casually, but you could tell he enjoyed being the star attraction.

"Well, we know what it looked like from the stands, but let's hear your version."

Steve launched into a long account of the game, and I stifled a yawn. Maybe it was the long walk on the beach, or the salt air, but I was unbelievably tired. Or maybe — just maybe — Steve was boring.

I felt a little guilty even thinking it, because he really seemed like a nice guy. *But not my type*, a little voice piped up inside. I looked at him, and tried to figure out what was wrong. He was about six-two — *a little taller than Jeff*, I caught myself thinking — and his hair was a shade darker. Jeff's hair was sandy, and — I was doing it again! Why was I comparing everyone I met with Jeff?

I took a deep breath and forced myself to be objective. I took another look. Steve had nice features, and had gotten dressed up to take me out. He had on a light tan sport coat, and really looked very attractive. If there was no magic, no fireworks, well, maybe once we left the house things would get better.

We finally made our getaway, and I had to admit I was glad to see that he had a nice car. A sporty number in silver and blue.

"You look very pretty," he said once we were in the car.

"Thanks." I smiled at him. *He certainly was polite*, I reminded myself for the dozenth time. If I was somebody's mother, I'd be crazy over him.

I took a peek at Steve. He really wasn't bad, I caught myself thinking. Jeff was terrific to be around, but he didn't exactly shower me with compliments. *That's because he thinks of you as a friend,* I told myself. *Not a girlfriend. Just a friend who happens to be a girl.* I was thinking about Jeff and wondering what he was doing when Steve broke into my thoughts.

"We can see a movie after dinner, if you'd like."

I had to yank my attention back to him. "A movie? Sure, that would be great." It would be more than great. It would be fantastic. We wouldn't have to talk to each other. It was obvious that Steve's flashes of brilliance were confined to the football field. A conversational genius he wasn't.

I was dredging my mind for something to say, when he piped up, "What kind of movies do you like, anyway?"

At least that was a start. "Oh, I like all different kinds. I like comedies — just about anything by Woody Allen —" I stopped when he groaned and shook his head. "You don't like Woody Allen?" I was amazed.

"His movies never seem funny," he said apologetically. "Maybe I just don't understand them."

"Oh." There didn't seem to be much to say after that. In a minute, I'd be asking him what his favorite color was. There was a long pause. "I like horror movies, if they're funny and sort of campy. You know, the kind you don't take seriously."

"Like what?" He looked mildly interested.

"Oh, the really off-the-wall ones. You know, my favorite movie of all time is *The Attack of the Killer Tomatoes.*" I waited for him to say something. He didn't. "It's about these tomatoes that go on the rampage and terrorize a whole town." I gave a little laugh to show how funny the whole thing was.

"No. It sounds crazy," he said flatly.

I sighed. "What kind of movies do you like, Steve?"

"Anything with a lot of action or adventure." He probably watches sumo wrestling on TV, I thought. "I like Westerns," he said, and gave me a hopeful look. "And war movies are good," he added.

"Hmm." I nodded and tried to look pleasantly interested. Westerns and war movies. It was going to be a very long night.

I should have known that Steve would like anchovies on his pizza. Somehow it fit.

I hate anchovies.

"We'll get half and half," he said. "Sausage and green pepper for you, and anchovies and mushrooms for me."

"Okay, thanks." I smiled at him. I was determined to have a good time if it killed me. At the rate things were going, it probably would.

The waitress took a long time taking the order. She kept getting the toppings wrong, and then she broke her pencil and had to get another one. I didn't mind. At least it delayed the moment when Steve and I would be staring at each other over the red checkered tablecloth. Trying to T-A-L-K.

"Well," he said, when she finally got it right and scurried back to the kitchen.

"Well," I said brightly. He looked at me, and I heard myself babbling on. "I'm really glad we came here. It's very nice." I looked around the room like I had never seen a restaurant before.

"Me, too." The ball was back in my court.

"Amalfie's sure gets crowded on a Saturday night."

"It must be their biggest night of the week." He nodded wisely.

"Friday is probably fairly busy too," I said thoughtfully. If I ever wanted to do a term paper on the restaurant business, I'd have a good head start. I was wondering if we'd have to cover week nights, too, when Steve said softly, "Very nice."

His eyes were fixed on a point over my left shoulder. When I turned, I saw the object of his interest. A slim blonde who looked like the had stepped out of a shampoo commercial. She had a light tan, and everything about her looked golden — her skin, her hair, her pale yellow dress. Normally, I wouldn't pay that much attention to what another girl was wearing, but these were unusual circumstances.

She was with Jeff Nichols.

I gulped and turned back to Steve. "Tell

me about football," I said quickly. Anything to get his attention off Golden Girl. *What if he knew her! And what if he invited her over to the table? A cozy foursome. . . . I* would die, I decided. Right there on the spot. They could blame it on the anchovies.

"Football," I repeated sharply, since Steve didn't seem to be responding. He reluctantly pulled his eyes away from the girl and back to me.

"Football?" he repeated stupidly. You could almost see the circuits in his brain, chugging painfully, trying to make the connection.

"Yes," I said desperately. "I've always wanted to understand it, but I've never had the right person to explain it to me. The right person like you," I said, in case he still didn't get the message.

"Well, I don't know how good I am at explaining it," he said, trying to sneak another look at Blondie. "I just play it."

He really was amazingly slow. "Just tell me what the quarterback does," I said. I gave a helpless little laugh. "I don't even understand that."

"Oh, well, that's the key position on the team," he said, suddenly all business. My instincts had been right. He couldn't resist the opportunity to talk about himself. "You see, the quarterback actually moves the ball," he want on happily.

I smiled and put on what Laura calls my Interested Look. I tried to see where Jeff and his date were sitting out of the corner of my eye. I didn't want to be too obvious, or Steve would start looking for them too. They must have gone into the adjoining room that had the jukebox, I decided. It was darker in there, and definitely more romantic. I felt something like a knife twisting in my stomach, and realized what it was. I was jealous.

"Now, just pretend that the salt shaker is the opposing tackle, and the napkin is the quarterback." I nodded to show that I understood. Steve had laid out an elaborate playing field with toothpicks and forks. I had no idea what he was talking about.

"Here we go, so watch carefully," he said. "They try a squeeze play, we move in fast, and — whammo! Look what happens to the other team." He chortled as the silverware came crashing down on top of the sugar bowl. "That's exactly the play the Miami Dolphins used when they played Dallas."

I couldn't think of a single thing to say, but it didn't matter. Steve thought I was speechless with amazement. "Now, there's another play they could have tried. Let's put the ball back on the twenty yard line and try something else. . . ."

He began patiently rearranging the pieces, and I let my mind wander. That was the one advantage of being with Steve. He didn't seem to need much in the way of feedback. As long as I didn't yawn, or interrupt, he seemed pretty content to talk to himself.

He was moving the salt and pepper shakers back and forth in a clumsy dance, when I saw them standing over us. Jeff and Blondie.

"Hi, Tracy." Jeff was smiling at me, completely at ease.

"Hi, Jeff." I tried to match his casual tone, but I didn't succeed completely. He was staring at the mess on the table, and I felt that I had to explain. "Steve's been explaining football to me." Anyone who didn't know me would think that I was spending the most fascinating evening of my life. "Steve, this is Jeff Nichols. Steve Richards."

"Hi, Steve." They both smiled, but you could tell they were sizing each other up. "And this is Diana Powers," Jeff said. *Diana. She was even named after a goddess.* I didn't stand a chance.

Steve forgot to be Mr. Cool and gawked at her. She was gorgeous. "Hello Steve." She had a terrific smile, and one of those low, sexy voices that I've always admired. It's a lot harder to do than you think. Whenever I try to sound sexy, people think I have a sinus condition.

"Diana, this is Tracy Evans," Jeff said. I was wondering when he'd get around to that. She barely nodded to me. She probably didn't want to strain that perfect voice.

Now that everyone had said hello, the conversation ground to a halt. The four of us stared at each other like we were waiting for a bus. I glanced at Steve, but his eyes were riveted on Diana. No hope from that quarter. Jeff was looking at me with an odd expression on his face. He didn't seem as embarrassed by the silence as I did.

"I think you and Tracy might have some classes together," Jeff said helpfully.

She gave him a "you've-got-to-be-kidding" look and turned her attention back to Steve.

"I don't think so," I said. I know I'd remember someone who looked like Diana.

"I really liked your moves in the last game," Diana said to Steve. He still hadn't taken his eyes off her.

"I'm glad. I've got plenty of others."

She laughed, and naturally it was low and sexy, too. "I bet you do."

"One large half and half," the waitress yelled. She banged down a steaming pizza on the table.

"We better be going, Diana," Jeff said. "Our pizza is probably waiting for us."

They moved off and I breathed a sigh of relief. I never thought I'd be so glad to see an anchovy pizza.

By the time we left Amalfie's it was too late to go to the movies, so we just decided to ride down to the pier and back. I was glad that Steve didn't suggest anything crazy like parking, but apparently, he didn't feel romantic toward me, either. Maybe it wasn't flattering, but I was grateful.

"Are you sure you don't want to stop for ice cream or something?"

I couldn't tell if he was being polite, or if he just had a big appetite. He had eaten most of the pizza at Amalfie's. I wasn't terribly hungry, especially after seeing Jeff and Diana. "No, thanks, really. I'm kind of tired, and I've got a headache, actually." I was dying to go home, but I didn't want to hurt his feelings.

"Hey, I'm sorry," he said, immediately contrite.

"It's not your fault." I smiled at him. "I think it was just the noise and smoke in Amalfie's."

He nodded. "It bothered me a little, too."

When we got to my front door, he gave me a quick kiss on the cheek. "Thanks for tonight, Tracy. Get a good sleep, and I'm sure you'll feel better tomorrow."

He turned to leave and I saw something glinting in the darkness. "Steve," I said suddenly, "what's that around your neck?"

"Oh, this?" He pulled out the chain and showed it to me. "It's a fish."

"A fish?" I said unsteadily.

"Well, it's really two fish. Swimming in opposite directions. It stands for Pisces. That's my sign. Pisces," he repeated proudly. "Good-night, Tracy."

I walked into the house in a daze. *You've been waiting for a sign*, the horoscope said. *Waiting for a sign.*

It also said today was the day.

The sign was Pisces. The sign meant Steve.

E^{ight}

"How'd it go, honey? You're home early."
Mom was curled up on the sofa watching the
late show.

"So-so." How could I explain that Steve
Richards was the most boring guy I had
ever met — even if he was supposed to be
destined for me!

"Steve has lovely manners," she said. "Dad
and Tom really enjoyed talking to him."

"Please!" I groaned and held up my hand.

"Sorry." She laughed. "I guess mothers
and daughters look for different things in
young men. By the way, I'm sorry I missed
meeting Jeff today." She had been out shop-
ping when he came by to get me. "Maybe
you'd like to invite him over for dinner some
night."

When I didn't answer right away, she
smiled. "Or is that too old-fashioned and

corny? Maybe girls don't bring their dates home for dinner anymore."

"He's not a date. . . ."

"I know. He's just a friend."

"Right." I was glad when the tea kettle whistled and she jumped up. I just couldn't face talking about Jeff. Not now. Not after I had seen him on a date with Diana.

I bet they're still out somewhere, I thought with a pang. Maybe at a movie, or dancing, or walking down by the river. Probably holding hands, and maybe even kissing.

Well, why shouldn't he go out with her? Or with anyone else he wants to, for that matter. If I were really his friend, I'd be glad that he was having a good time, wouldn't I? Maybe the book was right. Pisceans get too wrapped up with their feelings. I'd have to watch out for that. What I needed was to be cool and logical about the whole thing.

"It's been a slow evening here," Mom said, coming back with a tea tray.

The house was strangely quiet, and I realized what was wrong. I couldn't hear the computer going.

"Dad and Tom went over to someone's house to help them set up their new computer. You should have seen how excited they were." Mom smiled and shook her head. "I guess it's their idea of fun."

"I'm glad someone's having fun," I said. I was feeling sorry for myself again and I knew it. The trouble was, I couldn't seem to shake the sad feeling that had come over me since Amalfie's.

"Okay," Mom said. She poured out two cups of tea and handed me one. "Drown your sorrows in some Spiced Apple Delight, and tell me all about it."

I had to smile. Mom believes in herb tea almost as much as she does in bran. "Oh, it's nothing, really." I could tell I wasn't fooling her.

"Sure," she said and waited. She knew I'd weaken eventually.

"We ran into Jeff at Amalfie's," I blurted out. "And he had a date. A really goregous girl."

"Oh." She put her cup down and stared at me. "The plot thickens. Well, I won't ask the obvious question."

"Which is?"

"Which is, if you and Jeff are just friends, why do you care who he goes out with?"

"I've been asking myself that all night," I muttered.

"You went out with Steve tonight," she pointed out. "Did you expect Jeff to sit home and pine away?"

"No, of course not." I smiled. "He's not the type to pine away, even if I looked like Bo Derek."

"You like him very much, don't you?"

"Yeah, I do. And I can't explain it. When I'm with Jeff, I feel terrific. I can be completely myself, as if I had known him forever. And we're so much alike, you wouldn't

believe it." I grinned, remembering the to-
mato movie. "We love the same horror movies, and he even guessed that I liked peanut
butter and date sandwiches."

"He sounds like a very unusual boy," she
said, sipping her tea.

"He is."

She was silent for a moment. "Tracy, how
does he feel about you? Do you know?"

"Yes. I know, all right. He thinks of me as
a friend. That's it."

"You're sure?"

I nodded. "It's very obvious." I stood up.
"And there's nothing I can do to change it.
Nothing I should do," I added quickly. "It's
just not meant to be."

Every horoscope book in the world tells
you not to get involved with a Libra. I didn't
want to tell Mom that, or she might think it
was silly.

Plus, let's face it, when a boy is interested
in you romantically, he doesn't kiss you on the
nose. I didn't want to tell her that, either.

It was great to have Laura back at school.
We managed to get a table to ourselves in
the cafeteria, so we could catch up on everything.

"I feel like I've been out for a month, in-
stead of three days," she said. "I've missed
everything. Four couples have broken up,
Jerry Sherwood did something and now
Jenny Clayton won't talk to him, and Dick
Butler got suspended."

I stared at her in amazement. "You found out all that?"

She nodded. "Before first period," she said modestly. "I would have found out more, but Miss Wiggins accused me of loitering in the hall. But that's not important," she went on rapidly. "You're the one I really want to hear about. You and Steve. How did it go Saturday night?" She speared an olive and looked at me expectantly.

I told her, as briefly as I could.

"It sounds awful," she said when I finished. "Except I think you're reading too much into the part about seeing Jeff with Diana."

"You do?"

"Sure. You shouldn't get so upset over a thing like that."

"Wouldn't you?"

"Probably not. I'd do everything in my power to get him, though. If that was what I really wanted." Aries people can be remarkably determined, I remembered. "Anyway, maybe you were his first choice, but he gave up when you said you had to run home to get ready to go out. Maybe Diana was just an afterthought."

"She didn't look like an afterthought," I said. That was putting it mildly. If Diana was on a menu, she'd be the main course. I'd be strictly á la carte material.

"Are you still checking your horoscope every day?" Laura asked suddenly.

"I forgot to, today." There was something

in her voice that made me look up. "Why? Is anything up?"

She laughed, but I got the idea she was trying to cover up something. "Well, it's just . . . just a crazy string of coincidences, I guess." She paused and lowered her voice. "Sometimes it's a little scary how things turn out."

"What sort of things?"

She glanced at her watch. "I'll tell you in a couple of hours. I'll know for sure, then." She smiled mysteriously and stood up. "I've got to run, Tracy. I told Mrs. Thorpe I'd see her for a few minutes before history class."

"Okay, I'll see you later." There was something about Laura's tone that made me very uneasy. It just wasn't like her to be so secretive. I didn't have long to think about it though, because suddenly I had a new problem.

Jeff Nichols sat down across from me.

"You're brave." He grinned at me and I stiffened. He was more conceited than I thought! He probably thought I'd be in the depths of despair after seeing him with Diana.

"Not brave. Just smart," I said in a frosty voice.

He burst out laughing. "What's so smart about getting Beef Encore?"

"Beef Encore?"

He pointed to my plate. "The Wednesday special. Don't you remember your French? Encore means again. Beef again. Beef hash.

Now do you get it?" He was staring at me like I had lost my mind. "That's why I said you were brave," he said patiently.

"Oh. Oh!" If this was a cartoon, a light bulb would have gone off over my head.

"What did you think I meant?" He gave me a strange look.

"Nothing, I — I guess the Beef Encore warped my brain." I managed a smile. I poked at the gray meat. I had been so busy talking to Laura, I hadn't realized how awful it looked.

"What did you think of Amalfie's?" he said politely.

"The pizza's good," I said shortly, and took a swig of iced tea.

"Yeah, it is," he agreed. "I was surprised you ordered anchovies, though. You don't seem the type."

"Really?" I said coolly. "Maybe there are a few things you don't know about me."

"Maybe."

I looked at him and wished I hadn't. He looked terrific. Blue crew neck sweater and tan pants. He should always wear blue, I caught myself thinking. His sweater picked up the blue in his eyes, and . . . I killed the thought before it could go any further.

"I was kind of surprised to see you with Steve Richards. He doesn't seem like your type."

I couldn't believe it. First the anchovies, and now Steve. "How could you possibly know that?" I tried to sound very cutting and sarcastic, but it didn't seem to faze him.

He smiled. "Well, I haven't been here long, but I've heard a lot of talk about him."

"What kind of talk?"

He picked up a fork, played with it, put it down. "Enough to know he's not your type."

The bell rang then. "I've got to go to class," I muttered and dumped my tray. Jeff was right behind me. He pushed open the swinging door, and stood looking at me for a minute in the hall.

"I had a good time at the beach," he said softly. He touched my arm very lightly and walked away.

"It's strange. Very strange," Laura agreed. "It sounds like he's jealous."

"He can't be. We're just —"

She stopped me with a look. "I told you I was going to strangle you if you said that one more time."

"Sorry."

"Why didn't you ask him about the blonde — Diana? It was the perfect opportunity."

"I know. I should have said something, you're right. It's crazy, but he really put me on the defensive. For some reason, I felt like I should be apologizing for going out with Steve. None of it makes sense."

"Well, I'm just about to show you something that does. C'mon out to the kitchen with me."

I still didn't have a clue what Laura was

up to. She had acted really weird at school. When I saw her in the hall after lunch, she had whispered, "It worked!" She had a big smile on her face, like she had just discovered uranium, and wouldn't say another word.

"Okay," she said, opening up the refrigerator. "The moment you've been waiting for." She pulled out a plastic container and popped the lid. "Take a look."

I looked. "It looks like used chewing tobacco."

"Don't be silly," she said impatiently. "It's tea leaves."

I was baffled. "Why would you save tea leaves?"

"Because I've learned to read them." She laughed, and held them up to the light.

"This is a joke, right?"

"Oh, no, it's no joke," she said very seriously. "All the secrets of the cosmos can be revealed in the bottom of your cup. Or in this case, plastic container," she added. "You can ask any question, and the answer's right before your eyes. You can ask about boyfriends, or grades, or anything. Once you know how."

I stared at her. I finally figured it out. She was nuts.

"Uh, Laura," I began. I'd have to do this tactfully. "Do you remember when you sprained your ankle?"

"Well, of course I do," she said impatiently. "It was just last week, Tracy."

"What I'm getting at is . . ." I decided to start over. "Is there any chance you could have hit your head? Do you have headaches, or see double, or anything like that? You know, a lot of people have concussions, and don't even know it." Actually, I wasn't sure the last part was true, but I thought it sounded pretty good.

"Tracy, I don't know what's gotten into you, but I'm fine. In fact, I'm into taseology."

"Taseology?"

"The science of reading tea leaves. You notice I said a science."

"I noticed."

"Well, there's actually an art involved, too, but it does have a firm scientific basis."

"I'm sure it does. That's why we take tea-reading 101 right after biology every day."

"People always make jokes about things they don't understand," she said breezily. "Now," she said, very seriously, "ask me something you want to know."

"Laura. . . ."

"Just ask. I went along with your horoscope business, if you remember."

"I thought you didn't believe in it."

"I didn't. Not in the beginning. But then so many things started happening, that I wanted to investigate for myself. When I sprained my ankle I had plenty of time to read up on astrology. That's how I discovered taseology. It's not a substitute for astrology, it's an addition."

An addition. I had a headache just listening to her.

"I wouldn't know what to ask."

"Then I'll ask for you," she said briskly. "Now, the first order of business is to figure out Jeff. What's he going to do, and how does he really feel about you. Agreed?"

"Yeah, I guess so. Except I already know the answer."

"We'll see."

$N\underline{\underline{ine}}$

When I saw Laura at school the next day, she was still talking about taseology. "You know, Tracy, if you hadn't gotten me interested in horoscopes, I probably never would have investigated taseology." She looked at me very seriously. "Isn't it funny how things work out?"

"Very funny." I was only half listening to Laura, because I spotted Jeff coming out of math class. There was a familiar blonde head beside him, hanging on his every word, naturally.

Laura caught on. "Wow! Is that her?"

"I'm afraid so," I muttered. It was one thing to convince myself that Jeff and I were meant to be friends, and another to see him with another girl.

It was too late to duck down the corridor, so I pretended to be having a fascinating conversation with Laura. Laura played the game to the hilt.

"He did what?" she screamed with laughter. "Oh, Tracy, you're too much!" It's too bad they already gave out the Academy Awards, because she really deserved a nomination. "And then what happened?" She turned, right on cue, when Jeff and Diana reached her elbow. "Oh, hi, Jeff."

"Hi, Laura. Tracy." He smiled at us. "You remember Diana," he said easily. I nodded, but Diana stepped around me, like I was something squishy she had seen on the sidewalk. She turned her attention back to Jeff, and the two of them continued down the hall.

"So much for that," I said.

"The game's not over yet," Laura said mysteriously. "Since I've been reading tea leaves, I've learned never to give up too quickly. Things can change from minute to minute. If you want, I'll be glad to give you another reading today."

"Uh, thanks, but I think I'll stick to my horoscope," I told her. "I still have a lot to learn."

Mom was just about to throw the remains of her tea down the sink when I stopped her. "Wait, let me take a look."

"Honestly, Tracy." She shook her head and handed me the cup. "I can't imagine what you're doing."

"School project," I said hurriedly. There were a few tea leaves scattered on the bottom of the cup. I tried to remember the tips Laura had given me, but it was no use. I didn't see any pattern in them at all. They were just tea leaves.

"You've been acting kind of strange lately, Tracy," she said. "First you started grabbing the paper to read your horoscope, and now tea leaves?"

"It's just a hobby," I said. I looked around the kitchen, wondering where she had stashed the evening paper. I certainly didn't want to ask for it, after the crack she made.

She looked at me very seriously. "Tracy, you're not getting too wrapped up in all this fortune-telling, are you? I mean, it's fine for a game, or a joke, but. . . ." she let her voice trail off.

"Oh, I know there's nothing to it," I said. "I got interested because a few times my horoscope predicted things that really came true." I hesitated. "But I know that it's nothing more than a string of coincidences, like Jeff said. He feels just the way you do about it." I knew she'd like to hear that.

"I'm glad you said that." She smiled and tossed me a dish towel. "I've got two people in the family who are fanatics about computers. I don't think I could face it if you suddenly developed an obsession about something, too." We heard a shout of laughter from the dining room. Rick Jacobs and Tom were working on some new program.

"No fear of that." I gave a convincing laugh. "I know it's all just a game."

The minute she went into the den, I spotted the paper on top of the refrigerator. I yanked it down, and quickly turned to the horoscopes. Pisces, Pisces. I ran my finger down the page. Without even meaning to, I read the one for Aquarius.

Tackle that important project now and get the recognition you deserve. Tomorrow could be too late. Money and satisfaction can be yours.

Then I found what I wanted. Pisces. *Say yes when the signs are right. Don't spend your time dwelling on a fantasy, when a real-life opportunity is staring you in the face.*

I was still puzzling over it when the phone rang. I answered it, forgetting to put on my best "telephone voice." It didn't matter because it was only Laura.

"Have you read the paper?" she demanded.

"Just the horoscopes."

"That's what I mean." She sounded depressed. "What did you think of mine?" She gave an enormous sigh.

"Uh . . ." I stalled and flipped back through the paper. Aries. *Don't let appearances deceive you. Love can be as magical and mysterious as violets in the snow. Open your heart to it.*

I didn't see what she was so depressed about. "It's kind of strange, I guess."

"Kind of strange! It's insane. I wish I had never started reading these things," she grumbled.

"Laura, will you please calm down and tell me what's bothering you?"

"Okay. You're not going to believe this, but here goes. I read my tea leaves today, and got a real surprise."

"The boy of your dreams is going to appear at any minute," I teased her.

"Something like that."

"Hey, I was only kidding." I could tell she was really upset.

"And then the horoscope. I don't know, it's just getting to be too much."

I still didn't understand. "Laura, what's bugging you?"

"Not what, who. And the who is . . . Rick Jacobs."

"Wait a minute." I pushed open the dining room door very softly. I could see Rick with his Hawaiian shirt and loony grin, staring at the computer screen.

"He's here right now," I hissed. "What happened? I thought you got rid of him weeks ago."

"I wanted to but something always came up. I was always afraid to turn him down, so I just stalled it off. Anyway, he asked me out for Saturday night."

"So what's the big deal? Just tell him no."

There was a long pause. "Tracy . . . he sent me violets today. Violets!"

It finally sank in. "Oh, no." I took another peek at Rick. Violets or no violets, I couldn't let her go out with him. "Laura, don't you see it's just a coincidence? The violets don't mean anything. They can't!"

"Violets in the snow," she said miserably. "It's like it's written in the stars somewhere. I'm destined to go out with Rick Jacobs."

The idea was crazy, but I felt a funny little tingle run down my spine. Maybe there were cosmic forces at work. Forces that Laura and I didn't fully understand.

"What about the snow?" I demanded. "The horoscope mentioned violets in the snow." It wasn't much of an argument, but I was grasping at straws. "That part doesn't fit at all. It was sixty-five degrees out today."

"But it's probably snowing someplace," she insisted. "Maybe in the Rockies, or Minnesota."

I didn't have an answer for that one. "Laura, I don't know what to tell you to do," I said finally. "I admit that it looks like you're supposed to go out with Rick. . . ."

"I was afraid you'd say that." Her voice was so low I could hardly hear her. "I'll talk to you later, Tracy. I'm just too depressed to stay on the phone."

And without another word, she hung up.

I was just about to tackle my math homework when the phone rang again. Jeff? I wondered. No such luck. It was Steve.

"Hi, there." He had the same great voice, but now that I had gotten to know the whole package, there was no magic there.

"Hi, Steve." I tried to summon some enthusiasm. He was a football star, I reminded myself. Most of the girls in my class would be thrilled if he called them.

"I thought you might like to go to a movie this Saturday. I owe you one from last week, remember?"

I never expected he'd ask me out again, and I was caught off guard. I just assumed that he had had a lousy time too. "This Saturday?" I hesitated.

"Yeah. Unless you' d rather go somewhere else. I think there's a motorcycle race going on just over the state line."

What a choice. An evening with the Hell's Angels, or a Bruce Lee film. "The movie sounds good," I said finally.

"Hey that's great." He sounded so enthusiastic, I felt a little guilty. "I'll pick you up at seven."

At least he didn't like to talk on the phone much, I thought as I hung up. Jeff was just the opposite. We could talk for hours, trying to stump each other with crazy questions, making each other laugh. I sighed. Why was I thinking about Jeff all the time? It was crazy, and I'd have to make myself stop.

The paper caught my eye, and I looked at my horoscope again. *Don't spend your time dwelling on a fantasy.* That's exactly what I had been doing! It's funny, but the horoscope had been right twice today. First, with Laura, and her violets in the snow, and now with my crazy daydreaming. *Say yes when the signs are right.* Well, at least I had done that. I had said yes to Steve. And if nothing else, he was at least the right sign. A Pisces.

"So you're the one who took the paper! I should have known," Tom said. He had come up behind me so quietly, he made me jump. "I've been looking all over the house for it. I didn't do the crossword today."

I don't think Tom can sleep at night if he doesn't do the crossword puzzle. Being compulsive is a typical Aquarian trait.

"Did Rick leave?" I asked, handing him the paper.

"Yeah, a few minutes ago." He sat down at the kitchen table and started working on the puzzle. "We were going to work on a proposal for the science fair, but we ran into a snag. I thought I'd do the crossword and go to bed. There's plenty of time tomorrow to iron out the bugs."

I was getting a glass of milk out of the fridge, and my hand froze. "Tomorrow could be too late." I said it without meaning to. It just popped out.

"What?" he said absently. He was staring at the crossword and frowning.

"Tomorrow could be too late," I repeated. This time I was sure. "Let me see the paper a minute."

"Hey," he said. "I was just trying to think of the name of the captain in Moby Dick —"

"Ahab," I said quickly. I found the horoscope. "Tom, you've got to do the project tonight," I insisted. "It says so, right here in your horoscope. Look at it. Tomorrow could be too late!"

"Tracy, you're crazy." He laughed. "Do you really think that horoscope was written for me?"

I thought of telling him about the violets in the snow, and my "dwelling on a fantasy" but decided against it. He'd probably never understand.

Even an Aquarian could understand money, though, and I decided to appeal to his greed. "Tom," I said patiently, "you and Rick will get some prize money if you win the science contest, right?"

"Sure." He smiled. "It comes to about three hundred dollars, and we're gonna split it." He reached for the paper. "But there's plenty of time to work on the proposal tomorrow. I'm really wiped out tonight."

"No, you've got to do it tonight." I held the paper just out of reach.

"Tracy, we have two weeks to get the proposal in to Mr. Summers."

"Tom, please. Just trust me this once. Call up Rick, and tell him you decided to get it in tomorrow. I bet if you talk it over, you'll solve the problem."

He looked at me for a minute. "I don't know. We're doing a computer program, and it's pretty tricky. . . ."

"Just do it. I just have a feeling it's really important to get it all squared away tonight."

He sighed and got up. "Okay. You're crazy, but you're persistent. I'll call Rick. It's just to shut you up, though," he added. "Not because I believe in some dumb horoscope."

* * *

I started to get into bed, and then spotted the notebook lying on my nighttable. It was still blank. Maybe I wasn't cut out to be a writer, I thought. But I was a Pisces, wasn't I? And we were supposed to be the writers and poets of the universe.

"How do I love thee? Let me count the ways." I skimmed over the book of poetry by Elizabeth Barrett Browning. It must be wonderful to love someone like that, I decided. "To the height and depth of my being. . . ."

I wondered if I'd ever feel that way about anyone, and if they'd feel that way about me. And then, like a magnet, my thoughts returned to Jeff. Always Jeff. I missed seeing his crazy grin, laughing at his crazy jokes. I missed walking on the beach with him, trading trivia questions with him. I had never met anyone before who was so perfect for me! Correction: Who *seemed* so perfect for me. Because, obviously, if he really was perfect for me, he'd feel the same way.

I sighed and went back to the poetry book. The whole thing seemed insoluble. Jeff and Steve. One boy wanted to date me, one didn't. One was the right sign, one wasn't. One boy was exciting, and one just wasn't my type.

If only I could change everything around. Then I thought of Laura and Rick Jacobs and had to smile.

Fate was dealing her a lousy hand, too!

Ten

Maybe Laura would have become hooked on horoscopes and tea leaves anyway, but I felt a little like Dr. Frankenstein. I was the one who had first gotten her interested in astrology. I had created a monster.

"I don't make a move without checking the morning paper," she was telling a whole table of kids in the cafeteria. "You can ask Tracy. She's the one who really opened my eyes to everything. If they ever cancel the sun signs column, I'll be lost." She giggled, but she wasn't exaggerating. You could always see the tip of the newspaper peeking out of her notebook.

"You read your horoscope every single day?" Pat Hopkins asked. She raised her eyebrows slightly. Pat is vice president of the student body. She's a nice girl, but she's so cool and laid back about everything, that sometimes you feel like shaking her to see if she'll react.

"And I check the tea leaves, too."

Pat turned to me. "And you believe in these horoscopes, too, Tracy?" I could tell that my IQ had probably just dropped about thirty points in her estimation.

"Uh, well, yes, I do." I wished that Laura hadn't brought up the whole subject. Especially in front of someone like Pat who wants to major in math in college, and walks around with a calculator strapped to her purse. *She's probably an Aquarius,* I thought automatically.

"There must be thousands of people who get this paper every day," Pat pointed out. "They all read the same prediction. How could it mean something special to each one of them?"

Laura just smiled and dove into her chocolate marshmallow sundae. "That's part of the mystery, isn't it Tracy? If you understand everything about it, it wouldn't be so special. Don't you like having a little mystery in your life?"

"No I don't," Pat said frankly. "And if you checked the statistics, you'd probably find that only a small percentage of these predictions come true."

Laura sighed. "You sound very sure about it. But that's because you don't have all the facts. A lot stranger things have happened." Laura was smiling and I hoped she wasn't going to launch into the Rick Jacobs' story.

"And they're probably all coincidences," Pat said smugly. "You can have your horoscopes, but I'll stick to logic and numbers. At least you can always count on them." She stood up. "Are you ready, Norma? We've got a calculus test in six minutes."

"Is it that late already?" Norma Carsons looked up and moaned. "I've got another ten pages to get through." She had kept her eyes glued to her math book all during lunch. "You go ahead, Pat. I'll catch up." She gave a giant sigh, and went back to the book.

"You don't have anything to worry about, you know," Laura said a moment later. "I'm sure everything will turn out okay for you, Norma."

"It will?" Norma pushed a strand of hair out of her eyes and stared at her.

"Sure. You're a Capricorn."

"How did you know that?"

"Your birthstone ring." Laura smiled. "And this is a great day for Capricorns. You can see for yourself." She handed Norma the newspaper. "Halfway down the column."

"A pleasant surprise is in store for you. Don't worry needlessly about small details." Norma frowned. "I don't know. I wouldn't exactly call a calculus test a small detail."

"Trust me. You'll be okay."

The bell rang then, and we all got up. "I'm not sure it was a terrific idea to get into all the astrology stuff," I muttered to Laura. "Anyway, I don't think Norma's convinced."

"Oh, she will be." Laura gave a little laugh.

"And it would be silly not to share what we've learned with other people. Look how much astrology has helped us."

I nodded, but secretly, I was beginning to have my doubts. Maybe it was better not to know what was in store for you.

"You smell like formaldehyde." Jeff and I were crossing the school parking lot.

"How nice of you to say so." I pretended to glare at him, but it was no use. I was really glad to see him again. "I just got out of biology lab. That might have something to do with it."

"How did you do with Kermit II?"

"We got an A." I smiled, remembering the fun we had working side by side that day. "It was all because of you."

"I'm glad. I'd hate to think I'd lost my touch." He grinned, and I wasn't sure if he was still talking about frogs.

"That will never happen," I said wryly. Not as long as there are gorgeous girls around to fall all over him, I added silently.

"Are you going to join the film club?" he asked suddenly.

"The film club? I haven't even heard of it. Do they play classic movies or something?"

"You must not read the bulletin board," he chided. "They had a big announcement about it today. And it's the kind of club where you make movies, not just watch them."

"Really?" I was intrigued. I had heard that a lot of other schools had classes in film-making, but somehow Jefferson High had never come up with the money for the equipment. "Do you have to know a lot of technical stuff to join?"

"I hope not." He shrugged. "I don't know a dolly from a —"

"Doily," I finished for him.

"Hey, that's pretty good. Or you could say, a pan from a pain."

I groaned. "Some day I'm going to beat you at one-liners."

"But not today." He paused. "What do you say? Shall we sign up tomorrow?"

Sign up? For a moment, I was too startled to reply. Was this his way of saying that he'd like to see me? Why didn't he just ask me out! I had never in my whole life met anyone as puzzling as Jeff Nichols. Or as attractive, I admitted unhappily.

He was staring and grinning. "Is it such a tough decision? We've been blocking traffic for almost five minutes."

A car horn blasted, and I came to life. We were almost sideswiped by some kids in a van tearing out of the parking lot.

"Oh, I'm sorry," I said, feeling foolish. "I guess I was just thinking it over." We both stepped back on the curb.

"And. . . ." He was looking down at me, with those deep blue eyes, squinting a little against the sun.

"And I think it's a wonderful idea," I said weakly.

"Great! We can both sign up tomorrow. And now I'll give you a lift home. We'll stop for a soda first," he added, as if it was the most natural thing in the world. He wasn't in the least embarrassed that he hadn't called me in a couple of weeks, or that he was dating another girl. Like Steve, he just assumed that I'd be thrilled to see him, to be with him. The infuriating thing was that he was right. He put the top down on his VW bug, flipped on the radio, and gave me a big smile.

It must be nice to be a Libra, I thought enviously.

"I can't figure him out," I said to Mom. She had come home early from her public relations job, and I was glad.

"By him, you mean 'we're-just-friends' Jeff." She smiled and handed me a green pepper to dice. She had managed to find a store that stocked spinach pasta, and we were making a giant pot of spaghetti for supper. It smelled pretty good if you could just overlook the fact that it was green.

"Of course. Who else?" I shook my head and hunted for a knife.

"Well, you could be referring to Steve," she said reasonably. "Although, come to think of it, you've probably got him figured out already."

"Why do you say that?"

"Oh, I don't know. I guess he seems more

up front, less complicated than Jeff. With Steve, you know exactly where you stand. He certainly makes it clear how he feels about you."

That much was true. Steve had asked me out three weekends in a row. We had gone to a karate movie (that he loved and I hated), a Swedish movie with subtitles (that I loved and he hated), and a motorcycle race that was rained out. I couldn't for the life of me figure out why he kept on calling me.

And the fact that he was a Pisces was even more puzzling. We seemed to have nothing in common, except the stars kept insisting we were right for each other.

"What is it you don't understand about Jeff?" Mom asked, breaking into my thoughts.

"What he really thinks of me. It's so crazy!" I started chopping the green pepper a little more vigorously than I had intended. "First he acts like he's really interested. He spends a couple of hours in the lab cutting up Kermit for me, which couldn't have been a fun experience for him." I paused and slapped an onion on the counter. "And he surprises me with a kite, and we have a fantastic day together at the beach. Then the next thing you know, I see him out with Diana and it's like I've dropped off the face of the earth. I don't hear from him again. Not a word . . . until today."

"What happened today?" she asked softly.

"It was really strange. He came up to me

in the parking lot like nothing was wrong, and asked me if I wanted to join a film club. A film club! It's like a seesaw, back and forth, back and forth. Boys say that girls are hard to understand. Ha! I say just the opposite is true." I scraped the vegetables into the pot and added a little garlic.

"Tracy, there is one explanation that makes sense," Mom said slowly. She pushed her glasses back on her nose, and gave me a very serious look. "But I'm not sure it's what you want to hear."

"What is it? It couldn't be any crazier than the ideas I've come up with."

"It could be that you were right from the start." She shrugged. "Maybe . . . maybe he does just think of you as a friend. It would fit, you know. He thinks of Diana as a date, so he asks her out at night. But he thinks of you as a friend, someone he likes to be with. So he asked you to join the film club, so you can spend some time together. You said you have a lot in common."

"We do." I felt depressed just thinking about it. "You really think that's it?"

"Well, it would explain a lot of things, wouldn't it? And it wouldn't be so terrible, you know. It's nice to have a boy in your life who isn't a boyfriend." She laughed. "That sounds a little silly, but you know what I mean. I remember, I had a friend like that once. Marvin Nesbitt." She poured a cup of tea and sat down. "If it hadn't been for Marvin, I never would have made it through chemistry lab. And I helped him with Spanish. We had lunch together every day, and talked on the phone every night. I spent more time with him than I did with my girlfriends. We were pals, buddies, through and through."

"Whatever happened to him?"

"Gosh, I don't know." She ran her hand through her thick brown hair. "The last I heard, he married someone from Peoria and had six kids."

"Oh." I didn't want to hurt Mom's feelings, but how could she think that Marvin Nesbitt was anything like Jeff Nichols? They were worlds apart. Jeff was terrific, charming, and by far the most exciting boy I had ever met. And Marvin might have been great at chemistry, but he didn't sound like any girl's fantasy.

I was still puzzling over the whole thing when Laura called me right before dinner.

"We should open a consulting service," she said excitedly. "Norma just called, and she was thrilled. She didn't have to take the calculus test after all."

"What! Why not?"

"Because Mrs. Martin said that anyone who had over a ninety average in calculus could be excused, that's why. She had told the other class, but forgot to tell Norma's class. Pat was excused too, naturally."

"So all the worrying was for nothing," I said slowly.

"Right. One look at the horoscope would have saved them all that trouble. I've got to run," she said. "I'll call you later. I just wanted you to know that we were right after all."

"You were right after all," Tom said, sliding into the chair next to me.

"About what?" I said absently. I was still thinking about Jeff and the film club.

"About the computer project." He helped himself to an enormous portion of spaghetti. "When Rick and I got to school this morning, we found out that Chuck Robards was going to submit almost exactly the same thing. And you know that Mr. Holmes said there couldn't be any duplication."

"And so what happened?" I suddenly forgot to be hungry.

"Well, luckily, I took your advice, and I got most of the proposal done last night. I checked it over with Rick during study hall, and we got it in by ten o'clock. In other words, we beat Chuck. I still can't believe you came up with the idea."

Dad had been listening to the whole exchange, and leaned forward eagerly. "Did Tracy help you with your computer project, Tom?" Poor Dad had been trying to make a computer convert out of me for the past couple of years.

"Not exactly." Tom laughed. I tried to kick Tom under the table, but he went right on. "She read my horoscope, and decided that I had to get my computer project done last night. As it turned out, she was right. Today would have been too late. Pretty crazy, huh?"

"I didn't know you believed in anything like that, Tracy." He was frowning, and didn't look too thrilled at the idea.

"Oh, I don't," I said, making light of it. "I just, uh, happened to notice it that day, and thought it would be fun to tell Tom about it. It was just a lucky coincidence that it gave good advice." I smiled and attacked my spaghetti.

Dad looked relieved, and the conversation turned back to the Wonders of Computers. Mom gave me a sharp glance, but I just gave her my innocent look, and she gave up.

$E^{\underline{leven}}$

Laura would never make it as a spy. She likes to talk too much. Enemy agents wouldn't have to threaten her with thumb screws to get her to open up. All they'd have to do is smile and act interested, and she'd tell them everything she knew. Maybe it's because she's an Aries, but she just can't keep a secret. By the next morning, everyone in homeroom was whispering about Laura's amazing powers.

"Do you know she actually told Norma that she didn't have to take the calculus test?" Sherry Thompson was saying in an awed voice. "And there have been other things, too."

What other things? I longed to say. I decided right then and there that if Laura had told anyone about Jeff and Steve, I would kill her.

I jumped in quickly. "That's not exactly

the way it happened." I tried to sound as casual as I could. "You see, Laura showed Norma her horoscope yesterday, and —"

"She did more than that. She interpreted it for her!" Sherry said accusingly. "The whole trick is how you interpret it, you know." She glared at me, and I realized that she thought I was jealous of Laura's ability. "Anyway," she went on smugly, "there was something else. Something to do with a boy. . . ."

A boy! I gritted my teeth and waited for the next sentence.

"Hi," everybody," Laura said cheerfully. She slid into the seat next to me, completely unaware that she had only minutes to live.

"Tell us about the boy," someone prodded Sherry.

"Yes, tell us about the boy." I was looking right at Laura. "The boy and the horoscope."

"Oh that," she said lightly. "I think that was just a case of crossed signals." She gave a little laugh and avoided my eyes. "Anybody can have an off day, you know." The bell rang then, and she was off the hook.

"Did you say anything about Jeff?" I demanded the minute we were alone in the hall.

"Of course not." She looked surprised. "I was talking about myself. Violets in the snow, remember? I told them that my horoscope had matched me with someone . . . unlikely."

"That's putting it mildly," I said, starting to laugh.

"I know." She grinned. "Anyway, I didn't want to get into too many details. What if word ever got back to Rick?"

"If he thought you were destined to be together, there'd be no stopping him." I hesitated. "I still wouldn't say much about reading horoscopes, though. People might get the wrong idea."

"Don't be silly," she said. "It's not like we're setting ourselves up as fortune-tellers. Everybody can get the same information out of the paper themselves."

About three hours later, Laura's words came back to haunt me. It was nearly the end of sociology class, and I was finishing a first rate doodle of Mr. Stevens. He's very easy to draw, because he's tall and thin, with an Abe Lincoln beard. Sociology isn't my favorite subject, and I was letting my mind drift in and out as he lectured.

I was filling in the ears when suddenly I heard my name. Naturally, I snapped to attention.

"Since we have a resident fortune-teller in class, Tracy Evans, perhaps we could try a little experiment tomorrow." He looked at me with those piercing dark eyes. "Would that be convenient, Miss Evans?"

"Uh, sure," I gulped. I had the sinking feeling that he knew I hadn't been paying attention. *And how had he gotten the idea*

I was a fortune-teller? I didn't have time to worry about that, though, because he was obviously waiting for an answer. "What would you .. uh . . . like me to do, exactly?"

"Well, since we're working on personalities . . ." He paused, and made a church-and-steeple with his fingers. ". . . I'd like you to make some predictions."

"Predictions?" I warbled.

"Yes, predictions. We've seen how environment and heredity can influence personality, and I thought we should take a look at something different. Something really off beat. Tomorrow, let's see what astrology has to offer. Who knows? Maybe the secrets really are in the stars." He smiled, and I couldn't tell if he was serious or being sarcastic. He has what Mom calls a "dry sense of humor," which means that sometimes you don't get his jokes until two or three hours after you've heard them.

He stopped me as we filed out the door. "Bring any books or materials you want, Tracy. It should be an interesting class."

I smiled weakly, and shoved my way through the crush of bodies in the hall.

"Well, that's the price you pay for being famous." I turned around to catch Michelle Turner grinning at me.

"What are you talking about?"

"You mean you didn't see the school paper? Gee, I was going to ask you to autograph it for me," she teased. "Here, keep it," she said, shoving it in my hand. "I can get another copy."

The headline jumped off the page at me. NORMA CARSONS THANKS HER LUCKY STARS! My eyes skimmed the column. "A funny thing happened to Norma Carsons on her way to a math test. . . ." It went on to describe how Laura had read Norma's horoscope, and that the "prediction" had come true. "I never make a move without consulting my own horoscope," Laura was quoted as saying. "It saves a lot of time and energy."

"It must be a slow day for news," I muttered under my breath. Then my eye caught something else. "Laura says she owes her interest in astrology to Tracy Evans, an expert on the subject." *An expert!* No wonder Mr. Stevens had called me a fortune-teller.

I nabbed Laura after school. "What possessed you to give that crazy quote to the school paper? Don't you realize you're going to get us in a lot of trouble?"

"Honestly, Tracy, you worry too much." She smiled and shrugged. I should have remembered that Aries love publicity in all forms, and will do almost anything to get their name in the paper. "C'mon home with me. We'll have a diet drink and talk it over."

"Maybe later," I said shortly. "I've got to meet Jeff and sign up for the film club. I still don't understand why you mentioned me.

"Well, I owe it all to you," she said lightly. "I thought you'd want to take some of the credit."

I shook my head in disbelief. Sometimes it's just impossible for a Pisces and an Aries to ever understand each other.

"Well, I have to run," she said, glancing at her watch. "I told Rick I'd be home at three-thirty for his phone call."

"You're rushing home for a phone call from Rick?"

"It's not what you think." She lowered her voice. "I've got to think of a really fantastic reason why I can't go out with him this weekend." She sighed. "I've already used every excuse in the book. I was hoping you could help me come up with something."

"Sorry. My creative powers have dried up."

"Some Pisces," she teased. "You're supposed to be a writer."

"Some Aries. You're supposed to be good at getting yourself out of jams."

She stuck her tongue out at me. "Call me tonight, okay?" She winked. "I think we'll have a lot to talk about."

I didn't understand the wink until I turned to head back inside. Steve, Jeff, and Diana were walking straight towards me.

"Hi," Steve and Jeff said in unison. Diana, as usual, ignored me. "We just realized that all three of us are signing up for the film club," Jeff added. He was grinning as if he thought the whole situation was hysterically funny.

"And we better get a move on, or we'll be late," Steve added gruffly. He didn't seem at all amused.

I kept a foolish smile plastered on my face. "Great! Well, let's go." I felt ridiculous, but I was determined not to let it show.

We found seats in the auditorium, and I ended up between Diana and Steve. I caught myself sneaking looks at Jeff, who looked fabulous in a white tennis sweater, and tried not to look at Diana at all. She looked unbelievably bored, and I was wondering why she had bothered to come at all, when Steve leaned over to me.

"How about if you and I work together? We'd make a great team."

"Uh, sure," I heard myself saying. He had caught me totally off guard. I glanced at Jeff and Diana. They were talking intently, with their heads close together. It was obvious they were already a team.

"Do you have any idea of what we can pick as a topic? Let's pick something easy, and shoot it next weekend."

"A topic? Gosh, I don't know," I said absently. "I know as much about making movies as I do about computers." I laughed and then stopped. "Wait a minute. That could be a great topic."

"Computers?" Steve frowned.

"No, video games. My brother is practically addicted to them." I thought of Tom with his eyes glued to Defender and smiled.

"Yeah, video games might be a good topic," Steve agreed.

"You could film a video game room, and interview the kids," I said excitedly. "You could show them stuffing quarters in the machines, and find out why they like the games so much. In fact, you could even take a poll and find out what games are the most popular." Steve nodded and was going to say something, but Mr. Jordan bounded on stage just then, and started the meeting.

"You probably don't have much experience with moviemaking," Mr. Jordan started out, "but that's okay. We're all here to learn. If it makes you feel any better, I'm on trial, too. This is the first time I've ever offered a film workshop." This got a polite round of titters from the audience.

He spent the next half hour explaining and demonstrating the equipment we would be using. "A camera store donated some used cameras, and you'll each be responsible for buying your own film. Since you'll be working in teams, the cost will be divided two ways, so it won't be too bad." He paced restlessly across the stage with his hands clasped behind his back. "I don't think we need to get into a lot of technical details right away. It's strictly learn-as-you-go."

"How do we pick the teams?" a cute blonde in a jogging suit asked. I had been wondering the same thing myself.

He smiled at her. "You don't. I do." He held his hands up when there was a loud groan. "I know, you all want to work with your friends. But real life isn't like that. I went you to have the experience of working with strangers, even with people you might not like. So I'll pick the teams," he said firmly. "And I have a very simple system. I'm going down the rows and choose every other person — there will be two to a team." He got out a clipboard started calling out names.

I held my breath when he got to our row, but it didn't help. Jeff and I ended up as a team, and so did Diana and Steve. Jeff turned and gave me a slow smile. "Hi, partner," he said softly.

"He *what*!" Laura nearly choked on an Oreo. We were sprawled on her studio bed, along with a pile of pillows and stuffed animals.

"I told you," I said calmly. "He put Jeff and me on a team, and Steve and Diana on another one. I can't believe it. We'll be working together, seeing each other every day."

"It should be interesting," she said thoughtfully.

"I know." I took a sip of diet soda. "This stuff tastes terrible," I said. "Why do you bother drinking it, when you're eating cookies?"

Laura shrugged, unconcerned. "I don't know. I don't analyze everything the way you do. I'm an Aries, remember?"

"As if I could forget. I think I know more about your sign than I do about my own."

She sighed and changed the subject. "I don't suppose you came up with a life-long excuse why I can't go out with Rick, did you?"

I laughed. "I guess the truth would be too painful. I can't think of anything, unless you want to tell him you're allergic to Hawaiian shirts."

"Those shirts!" She shuddered. "I bet he glows in the dark. Not that I ever want to be in a position to find out," she added hastily. "Tracy, do you ever wonder why the horoscope made such a mistake about him? I mean, it really seems strange. It's been right about almost everything else."

"Maybe you really are destined for each other," I said very seriously. I ducked when she threw a stuffed giraffe at me. "No, I have to admit you're right. Rick Jacobs just wasn't one of our success stories. And Steve — there's another puzzle," I added.

"Most girls would love to go out with him, Tracy. He may not be right for you, but he's right for ninety-eight percent of the female population."

"I know, but according to all the signs, he's supposed to be right for me. It just doesn't make sense." I looked at my watch and scrambled to my feet.

"Do you have to go already? There's a good movie on TV."

"I need to get home and study some astrology. I don't know what Mr. Stevens has in store for me tomorrow, but whatever it is, I want to be ready." I grinned at her. "Thanks to you, my reputation is at stake."

Twelve

"I see you came prepared." Mr. Stevens was smiling as I dumped my books on my desk. The astrology book was right on top. Marlene Henderson glanced at the cover and snickered. "Oh, look, Lisa. She's going to tell fortunes."

"I can hardly wait," Lisa Hathaway replied in a bored voice.

"Maybe you and Lisa would like to be the first subjects," Mr. Stevens said to them, just as the bell rang.

Marlene's smile faded, and she and Lisa looked like they wanted to drop through the floor.

"Take your seats quickly, everybody. We've got a lot to do today. Tracy Evans is going to start with a short program on astrology. You've all heard of astrology, and most of you know what your sign is, right?" A little ripple of murmurs went around the room. "Good. Today we're going to put astrology to the test. Tracy is our authority." Thirty-two pairs of eyes swung toward me, and I tried to look unconcerned. "Using her knowledge of astrology, and her book, she's going to predict your signs. Okay?"

I took a deep breath. "I'll try."

"We have two volunteers in the front row" —that got a mild laugh — "and we'll start with them." Lisa and Marlene turned to me with nervous smiles pasted on their faces.

"Tracy, it's all yours," Mr. Stevens said. He took a seat in the back of the room, and I suddenly felt very alone.

"You want me to predict their signs, right?"

"Precisely."

"Okay. I'll start with Lisa." I tried to sound a lot more confident than I felt. Lisa was a bubbly blonde. I guess if you had to sum her up, you'd say she was a typical cheerleader. She was always enthusiastic, had a great smile, and about a dozen boyfriends. Her greatest worry was probably which pair of designer jeans to wear every day. She looked at me uncertainly, and I wondered where to begin. I idly thought of cheating, and looked to see if she was wearing a birthstone ring. No such luck.

Maybe Mr. Stevens sensed my hesitation, because he spoke up. "Tracy, you've known most of the kids for a year. All I want you to do is ask them a few questions, and then tell us what sign they belong to. That's the way astrology works, isn't it? Different personalities go with different signs." He was smiling a little, and I was pretty sure that I was being set up.

"Yes, that's right." If he was playing a game, I was determined to go along with it. And win.

"Then what are you waiting for?" he said mildly.

"Uh, nothing," I stammered. I took a deep breath. It should be a cinch to figure out what sign Lisa was. I took another look at her. It was all there. She was attractive, charming, and a real flirt. She loved music and sang in the choir. She laughed a lot, and she had a great sense of humor.

I ticked off the possibilities. An Aries? No, the drive, the ambition wasn't there. She wasn't determined to succeed like Laura was Maybe a Libra? No, she wasn't *that* much of a flirt. She had been going steady with Ron Phillips ever since freshman year. That would seem like a lifetime to a Libra.

"We're all going to grow old waiting for your verdict, Tracy," Mr. Stevens said. *Some dry sense of humor!* A few kids giggled, and I knew I was losing credibility fast. I'd have to be right on this first one. I just had to!

I rapidly went through the list. There was only one real possibility after all. "She's a Cancer," I said firmly. As soon as I said it, I realized my mistake. Lisa gave a silly giggle, and I felt like biting my tongue. She'd never be self-sacrificing enough to be a Cancer. Lisa believed in looking out for number one.

"You're wrong!" she chortled. "I'm a Capricorn!" She looked at Mr. Stevens triumphantly, as if she expected to get a prize. Mr. Stevens scratched his beard thoughtfully. He didn't look too surprised. "Well, you struck out on the first try, Tracy. But let's see how you do with Marlene."

I still couldn't believe it. *A Capricorn!* Isaac Newton was a Capricorn. It seemed impossible that he and Lisa could have the same sign. Lisa was nice enough, but she certainly wasn't an intellectual giant. I knew for a fact she had squeaked by algebra with a C minus, and that was only because her boyfriend did all her homework for her.

I approached Marlene more cautiously. She was the the studious type, always punctual, a straight A student. I tried to remember what the yearbook had said about her. She dreamed of going to dental school, she belonged to the computer club, she collected antique coins. This time there was no question.

"Taurus," I said flatly. *Please be a Taurus,* I whispered silently.

Marlene turned to Mr. Stevens and grinned. "I hate to say it, but I'm a Scorpio."

This time the whole class broke up. Mr. Stevens even allowed himself a little smile. "That's two out of two, Tracy. Is something wrong?"

"I . . . I can't understand it. It usually works."

"You seem surprised that Marlene is a Scorpio." *Surprised! I was amazed.* "May I ask why?"

"Scorpios are very mysterious and complicated," I said automatically. "They're capable of dark passions."

I had barely finished the sentence before someone in the back row hooted. "Dark passions!" I could feel myself turning a fiery red, and looked helplessly at Mr. Stevens.

"Let's try a few more," he said mildly. "You can start with some of the boys, Tracy."

The rest of the hour was a disaster. I thought that Cliff Morgan, star jock, was a Pisces, and he was a Sagittarius. And I was positive that Troy West, who had dated every single girl on the Senior Court was a Leo, but he turned out to be a Virgo. I guessed wrong every time. And to make things worse, I asked everyone a lot of questions about themselves before I decided. I probably could have done better by flipping a coin.

Just before the hour was up, Mr. Stevens took his place at the front of the class. "I didn't mean to put you on the spot today, Tracy," he said with a smile. "But I think our little experiment today speaks for itself. Horoscopes might be fun, but as a guide to personality, or behavior . . . well, let's just say, it's not in the cards. That's a little joke," he said, and everyone groaned. "Everybody read the next twenty pages for tomorrow, and we'll have a chapter test on Friday."

I could hear a few giggles as the kids filed out, and I pretended to be busy getting my papers together. I looked up to see Mr. Stevens looking at my astrology book.

"I hope I didn't embarrass you, Tracy. You know I can never resist an experiment."

"That's okay." I wasn't thrilled at being the class clown, but there wasn't much I could do about it. "Did you think things would turn out this way?"

"I'm afraid so." He tapped the book. "The only people who benefit from astrology are the ones who write these books. But I guess you don't need me to tell you that."

He was beginning to sound like my father. Cool and rational. Predictable. *He probably trusts his head instead of his emotions,* I decided. An Aquarius. I started to smile.

"What's so funny?" He looked a little startled.

"I'm sorry, it's just that . . . Mr. Stevens, has anyone ever told you that you're a perfect Aquarius?"

He started to smile then, too. "Yes, as a matter of fact, someone has. My wife." Another class started crowding into the room, and he lowered his voice. "But just because you guessed this one right, it doesn't mean anything, Tracy. Remember, it's just coincidence. Sheer coincidence."

"Oh, of course," I answered. "Don't worry, Mr. Stevens. I won't read too much of it."

I suddenly felt a little better.

"Hi, Tracy." "Hello, Tracy." Steve and Jeff were starting to remind me of Tweedledum and Tweedledee. You couldn't have one without the other. And Diana.

"Ready for film club?" Jeff smiled down at me, and I felt myself wishing that we were miles away from Jefferson High. Just the two of us, without Steven trailing like a shadow. *Don't be silly. He doesn't want to be alone with you. He has Diana waiting in the wings for him,* I reminded myself. *Once this film project is over....*

"Sure," I said. The four of us found seats near the stage and tried to find something to talk about.

Mr. Jordan hurried down the aisle a few minutes later, handing out mimeographed sheets. "Sorry about this, everyone, but I've got an appointment I just can't cancel. I'm going to turn you loose today." There was a chorus of groans, and he held up his hand for silence. "We're not canceling class." He smiled. "This is what's called independent study. You need some time to get to know your partner, and to choose your subject. Remember, you're making a five-minute documentary, so pick something that you can relate to. Something you feel good about, that you're interested in. Then I want you to plan your strategy. What's the best way to get your message across? Ask yourself what words, what images, will convey your feelings about the subject."

All the while he was talking, he was passing out dozens of sheets. I glanced at one and was immediately bored. It was a maze of numbers and diagrams — everything about lenses and F-stops to camera angles. There was obviously more to making a film than pointing the camera. "If you have any questions, hold them till the next class. In the meantime, divide up into pairs, and talk things out." He grinned. "That's what team work is all about. And remember, you have to hand me an outline before I can issue you the camera. It's first come, first served."

"It sounds so romantic. You and Jeff ended up together, after all."

Sometimes Laura's imagination runs wild. "It's not romantic at all," I told her. "It just worked out that way because of where we were sitting. I told you. That's the way Mr. Jordan chose the teams."

"Maybe." Laura shook her head. "I still think there's something funny going on. You said Jeff asked you out for a Coke again. It sounds like he wants to be with you."

"I told you. He didn't have any choice. It wasn't a date. We had to discuss the film project. Steve and Diana got together, too."

"I think that Jeff wanted the two of you to be on the same team," Laura said. "It's like he's going out of his way to throw the two of you together. If he wanted to be with Diana, why did he bother to tell you about the club in the first place?" She munched on a chocolate chip cookie and handed me the box.

"I wondered about that, too," I said. "It doesn't make sense, does it?"

"Is he still dating her?"

"I'm sure he is." I shrugged. "At least he's not seeing me, and I can't imagine him spending all his Friday and Saturday nights at home." I suddenly remembered something. "What did you decide to do about Rick Jacobs, the love of your life?"

She made a face. "Please! Not while I'm eating. I'm still stalling him." She laughed. "You wouldn't believe how many excuses I've come up with. I really should have been born a Pisces. I have a great imagination," she said modestly.

"You do fine as an Aries," I told her. "I think you'd be too exhausting as a Pisces. Anyway, I'm not sure that Pisces always have writing ability." I thought of my blank note pad still lying on my nighttable. At the rate I was going, I'd be forty by the time I autographed my first book of poetry.

"What are you doing this weekend?" Laura asked.

"A movie with Steve on Friday night, and I'm not sure about Saturday."

"It sounds exciting," she said politely.

"It isn't, unless black belts turn you on," I said gloomily.

She looked at me blankly.

"They're having a marital arts film festival."

"Oh." She shook the box of cookies. It was empty. "By the way," she said brightly, "you never told me how everything went in Mr. Stevens' class. Did you wow them?"

"Believe me, Laura, you don't want to know."

"C'mon, I bet you're just being modest."

"I bet I'm not."

She looked at my face and realized I wasn't kidding. "I think this calls for some ice cream," she said, scrambling to her feet. "Don't go away. I want to hear the whole story." She grinned. "I love tragedies."

_T_hirteen

"A double _yoko geri keage_ followed by a jump kick. I've never seen that before, have you?" Steve jabbed my arm excitedly. His mouth was open and his eyes were glued to the screen.

"Never," I said wearily.

"You don't seem to understand, Tracy. It takes years of practice just to do a single _ushriro geri keage_." He tore his eyes away from the movie long enough to glare at me. "And the guy moves like lightning. That skill is something you almost have to be born with. I've seen lots of black belts who can't even come close to him."

"Mmm." I chewed some ice chips, and wondered how much longer the show would last. I sneaked a look at my watch. For the past hour and a half, we had watched the hero single-handedly destroy an army of people in black pajamas. I had no idea why. I couldn't figure out what the plot was, but it had something to do with a shipment of opium and a beautiful Russian spy with a New York accent.

"Steve. . . ." I said softly.

"Just a minute," he hissed. He was literally sitting on the edge of his seat. "Watch what happens next. You're not going to believe this."

He dug his fingers painfully into my arm, and I looked at the screen. A little man with a ferret face was dangling from a helicopter. The camera zoomed in for a closeup as his fingers slowly started to lose their grip. First the thumb, then the pinkie. He was holding on by three fingers when suddenly a shadow crossed the screen. It was someone's foot. I felt a little sick, knowing what would happen next.

"Steve . . . I'm dying for a drink."

"Yeah, in a minute. This is the best part of the whole movie." I sighed and looked at the screen. The foot inched forward.

"I'm really thirsty," I whispered. I waited a whole minute, counting silently to sixty. "I'm going to get a drink," I said finally. Either he didn't hear me, or he was too absorbed to care, because he didn't even bother answering. "Okay?" I leaned over close to him.

He was gripping the armrests so tightly his knuckles were white. "Yeah, sure," he grunted. "Go ahead."

I sighed and got up. The lobby was empty

and I bought a drink from a yawning girl about my own age. I looked at some ads for coming attractions, stalling for time. From the squeals I heard from the theater, the foot had found its mark.

"Now there's a movie I can see over and over," I heard a familiar voice say. "I never get tired of it, do you?" I forced myself to turn around slowly. Jeff was staring at a giant poster for *Gone With the Wind*. "It really has everything," he went on. "Adventure, passion, a great plot. It's one of the classics, don't you agree?" He looked at me then, flashing a big smile.

Somehow I managed to find my tongue. "Yes, it is. I never can resist a love story," I said, with what I hoped was the right touch of sarcasm.

"Oh, yeah. That, too." He grinned at me. I noticed he was holding two drinks and two boxes of popcorn. Unless he had suddenly developed a tremendous appetite, he was with a date. "Are you, uh, waiting for someone, or just taking a breather from the show?"

I gave in and smiled at him. "I'm taking a break. I just couldn't face any more karate chops."

"I know what you mean. Diana really loves this kind of stuff, though. Did you know she's an orange belt in karate?"

"No, I didn't." *But I'll tuck that fascinatin bit of trivia away in my memory banks.*

He shifted his weight, and said, "Well, I

guess the drinks are getting warm and the popcorn is getting cold. And I don't want to keep you from. . . ."

"Steve," I said flatly.

"Steve." He smiled, and it was impossible to know what he was thinking. We both walked back into the theater, and I made it a point not to look where he was sitting. So much for that!

I sat down next to Steve, feeling more discouraged than ever. Why was it so depressing to see Jeff with someone else? And not just anyone else, but the fabulous Diana?

Steve was still staring raptly at the screen. "There's another good part coming up," he whispered. I looked up, and immediately wished I hadn't. One of the villains was doing a slow underwater dance with a shark, and it was obvious that the shark was leading. The water turned a suspicious pink color, and I nearly gagged.

I peeked at my watch again. "Something wrong?" Steve whispered out of the corner of his mouth.

"Oh, no," I said lightly. "I just noticed that the movie will be over in half an hour."

"Yeah, but don't worry." He reached over and patted my arm reassuringly. "It's a triple feature."

"What a night," I said softly, the moment I closed the door.

"That bad?" Mom was standing in the foyer, smiling.

"You can't imagine." I followed her into the kitchen, and sank into a chair. "I don't suppose there's any of that chocolate cake left, is there?"

"You're in luck. I saved you a piece. Tom was looking for it, but I figured this was an emergency." She handed me the cake and a glass of milk and sat down.

"How did you know?" My mother can read my moods like a barometer, but I didn't think even she could predict an evening like this.

She laughed and pushed the newspaper at me. It was opened at the horoscope page. "You've even got me reading these things, Tracy. I looked at it after dinner, and it said that tonight would be an absolute disaster for you."

"It did?" I grabbed the paper. *Pisces. Don't make plans to socialize this evening. A bitter confrontation could occur before midnight.* I read it slowly, twice.

"Well, did you have a bitter confrontation tonight?" Mom asked.

"I don't know if it was bitter, but it was disappointing," I said. I told her about seeing Jeff in the lobby.

"I'm surprised he was there. It doesn't sound like the kind of movie he'd like," she said thoughtfully.

"It isn't. He took Diana, and that's the kind of movie she likes. She's got an orange belt in karate."

Mom smiled. "You know what's funny? It sounds like Steve and Diana are the ones who should be going out together. They seem to share the same interests, just like you and Jeff do."

She was going to say something else, but Tom wandered into the kitchen then, and slumped into a chair. He spotted the paper, and made a face at me. "So much for your horoscopes," he said.

"What do you mean?"

"Remember the science project I was doing with Rick?"

"Of course I do. I tipped you off so you could get your proposal in a day early. I probably helped you win the award," I said modestly.

"That's what you think!" he snorted. "I just found out that Sandy Phillips won the award. They extended the deadline for proposals by a whole week, so she had all that time to work on it."

"Oh." I couldn't think of anything to say.

"Well, It's not Tracy's fault they extended the deadline," Mom said, jumping in. "Nobody could have predicted that would happen."

"No, but she could have minded her own business," Tom said darkly. "If Rick and I had had a whole week to work on our proposal, we would have had a much better chance. Instead, we rushed to get it in, because some crazy horoscope said we should.

It's a good thing you don't have to make your living telling fortunes," he added as a parting shot.

For a moment, no one said anything. I hated to admit it, but deep down, I knew that Tom was right. I should have minded my own business.

I crawled into bed, glad that the day was finally over. The episode with Tom had been the last straw. The stars *hadn't* always been right, I decided. Just before I went to sleep, I let my mind drift over the past weeks. The stars had been right some of the time . . . like the day I dropped Kermit down the sink and when I forgot we were having class pictures taken. And the day Laura's horoscope had warned her to be careful and she sprained her ankle in gym class.

But on the minus side, there was that embarrassing day in sociology class when I couldn't predict anybody's sign. And as far as boys were concerned, things were really confused. I smiled, remembering Rick Jacobs and the "violets in the snow." Rick and Laura — that had to be a foul-up!

And what about Jeff and Steve? Jeff was wrong for me, according to the stars, and Steve, a Pisces, was right. Yet, Steve and I had nothing in common, and Jeff and I. . . . I finally gave up and drifted off to sleep, with things more unsettled then ever.

"Anybody calling you at this hour must

be really devoted," Mom said sleepily. "On a Saturday morning!"

I sat up and blinked, trying to wake up. The bedside clock said seven. "Who is it?" I said foggily, stumbling out of bed.

"A boy," she said, as if that explained everything.

I dragged myself to the phone, puzzled. It had to be Steve or Jeff.

"Hi," I said, sounding like a frog.

"I know it's early," Jeff said cheerfully, "but I thought we could get an early start on the film project."

"The film project?" My tongue felt fuzzy and I could hardly wrap it around the words.

"Have you had breakfast yet?" He laughed before I could answer. "Probably not, judging from the way you sound. I'll pick you up in half an hour."

"Half an hour!" I sputtered, suddenly coming to life. "That's still only seven-thirty —" I was going to say more, but a long dial tone stopped me. He had hung up.

I dashed into the shower, and ran the water as hot as I could stand it. My mind was foggy, and I wanted to be at my best when I met Jeff. Why had he called me today? He hadn't said a word about last night — as if it was the most natural thing in the world for us to run into each other with dates at a movie. *It is the most natural thing in the world — that is, if you're only friends,* I reminded myself. *Darn! When would I learn to accept that?* I wondered.

Fourteen

"Why do I get the feeling you're not a morning person?" Jeff said cheerfully. He was working his way through a mountain of bacon, eggs, hash browns and pancakes. My stomach turned over lightly, and I tried not to look when he poured maple syrup over the whole thing.

"Do you know what time it is?" I answered, stifling a giant yawn.

"Eight-thirteen," he said seriously. "Isn't that terrific? We've got the best part of the day still ahead of us. You've heard that old cliché about the early bird."

"I didn't know we were chasing worms," I said wryly. I glanced around the Sugar Shack. It was nearly deserted. "I'm sure you have a wonderful reason for dragging me out of bed so early." I paused and sipped some scalding tea. It helped a little, but not much.

"I do," he said, waving his fork. "I figured we'd get the jump on everyone else today. Last night I was doing some thinking about your idea for our project. . . ."

"My idea?" I said slowly. *What in the world was he doing thinking about a film assignment when he was with Diana?* I was starting to feel more confused than ever.

"Yeah, your idea for the video game film. The more I thought about it, the more I liked it." I must have looked surprised because he grinned. "Well, I had to think about something during that awful triple feature."

I smiled at him. "I have to admit that I let my mind wander a bit, too."

"Let's face it," he said with a laugh. "We're just not cut out to be ninjas."

"I guess not."

Neither one said anything for a minute, and then he was suddenly back to business. "Anyway, I thought we should get an early start," he said briskly. He spread out some papers on the table. "I jotted down a rough outline of what you told me, and if it's okay with you, I thought we'd take it over to Mr. Jordan."

I looked at the neatly typed papers. "Uh, sure," I blurted out. "I'm really impressed. You've done a lot of work on this."

"Does that surprise you?"

"Maybe a little," I admitted. "I guess I didn't think you'd take it this seriously." *Especially since you missed the chance to work with Diana on it,* I felt like adding.

"Of course I take it seriously," he said, looking into my eyes. "I'd take anything seriously as long as you and I were working on it together. I always said we'd make a good team, didn't I? Remember Kermit?" He let his hand rest lightly on mine for a minute. "I really enjoyed that day together in the lab."

"So did I. I'm not sure I want to do it again, though." I laughed. "I've sworn off frogs for life."

"You're right. I think we can find better ways to spend our time." *Better ways to spend our time! What was he getting at?* I waited, wondering if he'd say more, but he just smiled and stood up.

"Like making films?" I prompted him.

"For starters." He looked down at me for a long moment and I had no idea what would happen next. "Tracy, I just wanted to tell you. . . ." he began.

"Yes," I said. We were standing very close together in the aisle.

"That is, I just wanted to say. . . ."

"Coming through!" a waitress yelled in my ear. She brushed past us, carrying an enormous tray. Jeff rolled his eyes at me.

"Yes?" I repeated.

He sighed and put some money on the table. "I think we better hurry so we can catch Mr. Jordan."

"Right." I took a deep breath and let it out slowly as he held the door for me. As usual,

Jeff was completely unpredictable. *A typical Libra trait,* I reminded myself.

"Well, I like your idea, kids, but someone else is already using it."

"They are?" Jeff and I looked at each other in surprise. "I thought we'd be the first ones to see you today."

Mr. Jordan smiled. "Steve Richards beat you to the punch, I'm afraid. He and Diana Powers were here a few minutes ago, and they turned in an outline." He picked up a sheet of paper and glanced at it. "The funny thing is, it sounds almost identical to yours."

"What a coincidence," I said sarcastically. I could feel my face getting red, the way it always does when I'm mad.

Mr. Jordan shot me a puzzled look. "It certainly looks that way." He glanced at his notebook. "Let's see, Steve and Diana are going to interview kids at a video game room, find out what the most popular games are, and see how much money kids spend on them." He stopped and looked at me. "Is that what you and Jeff had planned?"

"That's exactly what we had planned." *What a rat!* I thought to myself. I had to bite my tongue from saying it out loud. It's bad enough Steve didn't have any ideas of his own. He had to steal mine.

Jeff spoke up, then. "That's okay, Mr. Jordan. I've got another topic we can use." He looked at me. "That is, if it's okay with Tracy."

"Let's hear it," Mr. Jordan said, sitting on the edge of his desk.

"I'd like to do a film on the beach," Jeff said quickly. "No narration, just some music. We could call it 'A Day at the Beach,' and we'll include shots of all the things you can do there. Like flying kites, having a picnic lunch, wading in the surf." He turned to me. "How am I doing so far, Tracy?"

"You're doing great." I couldn't believe he came up with something so fast. "But do we need to put it all down on paper, Mr. Jordan? Jeff and I had hoped that we could get started on the filming today."

"Let's make an exception this time," he said thoughtfully. "After all, you did have an outline ready to turn in. It's not your fault if someone else is using it." The way he said it made me suspect that he knew exactly what Steve had done. "So go to it." He grinned and handed me a camera. "Have fun, you two."

"What was that all about? You look furious." Jeff opened the car door for me, and waited while I slung some of the equipment on the back seat.

"I am furious! That rat stole my idea. Word for word!"

"What rat?" He was grinning as if the whole thing was a big joke.

"Steve Richards. And you know darn well who I mean," I said, glaring at him. "Steve asked me that very first day in film club if we could work together. When I said yes, he asked me for a good topic, and I told him my idea for the video game documentary. I never thought he'd steal it!"

"Gee, I'm really surprised he'd do that," Jeff said innocently. "That's kind of strange behavior for a Pisces, isn't it? I thought they were supposed to be trustworthy and reliable, not dangerous like us Libras." I looked at him, but he kept his face very serious.

"Yes, I guess it is a little strange." I rolled down the window, and Jeff started the car. It was a beautiful day, and you could feel the warm breeze rolling in from the ocean. "It's just lucky that you had another topic ready," I said in a softer voice.

"It sure is. Life is full of surprises, isn't it?" Jeff was grinning at me, and I forgot that I was supposed to be furious. In fact, I suddenly realized that I was enjoying myself too much to worry about anything.

We didn't talk much as he drove along the narrow road that led down to Palmer's Beach. "Well, this is it," he said, pulling up to a shady spot. He swung his long legs out of the car and unloaded the equipment. "Hollywood, here we come."

"I hope you know what you're doing," I muttered, as I unpacked a box of lenses.

"Oh, I know exactly what I'm doing, Tracy. That's one of the nice things about Libras, you know. They're always in control. But then, I don't need to tell you all this. You're the astrology expert." He swung the camera pack over his shoulders and put his arm around my waist as we headed down the beach. If I didn't know better, I would swear it was turning into a real date, not just a film project. I stared at him and didn't know what to say. Nothing was working out the way I had expected!

If I thought I would feel uncomfortable working with Jeff, I was wrong. We immediately started cracking jokes and one-liners, as we loaded the camera. I was glad Jeff had thought to bring film. I had completely forgotten about it.

"Okay, I've got one for you. What's Shazam's real identity?" Jeff was grinning from ear to ear.

I groaned. "Billy Baxter. And don't bother me with such easy ones," I teased him. He started to set up some shots of me walking along the beach.

"I've got another one," he said, snapping his fingers. "Okay, how about this. What's Princess Leia's home planet?" He squinted through the camera at me, as I picked up a conch shell. "Yeah, that looks good. Just keep looking at the shell, while I check the exposure."

I pretended to be lost in thought. "Uh . . . I think it's . . . I mean, could it be . . . Alderaan?"

"You knew it all the time," he said reproachfully, and made a face at me. "You're the world's champion trivia expert, aren't you?"

"Yes, but I'm too modest to admit it." I

146

sighed. "You're just not in my league, Jeff."

He held the light meter up to my face, and ran his finger lightly over my cheek. "We'll see about that," he said in a husky voice. "But first, we have a movie to make."

"I can't believe it," I said, unwrapping the peanut butter and date sandwich.

"You haven't lost your taste for them, have you? Because there's always corned beef on rye."

"No, I still love them." I smiled at him. "I'm just amazed that you'd remember a crazy little thing like that."

"Oh, I remember everything about you," Jeff said. "I remember the last day we spent here." He sat down on the sand next to me. "I remember how cute you looked chasing that kite I gave you, and the way your hair looked in the sunlight. . . ." he leaned over and brushed a lock of hair out of my eyes. "I knew we'd come back here some day."

"You did?" I started to take a bite of my sandwich and stopped. "How? I mean, why?"

He laughed and slid his arm around me. "Oh, I don't know. Call it fate, or destiny, or something. I just knew we would." He paused. "And here we are."

I was starting to feel a little nervous, because he was looking so intently at me. "Here we are. . . ." I said with a little laugh. "Anything else you remember?"

"Mmm hmm." He touched the tip of my nose. "I remember a girl who swears we were meant to be friends. Just friends."

"Well, that's true, isn't it?" I said, returning his stare. My heart was doing a funny little flip-flop, but I was determined not to back down now.

He nodded. "It's true," he agreed. "We're meant to be friends . . . but so much more." He leaned over then and gave me a real kiss.

When we finally came up for air, I stared at him. "You've always felt this way about me?"

"Definitely," he said, nuzzling my cheek. "I knew it from the start." He laughed. "But I also knew it would take a lot to convince you."

"You mean you planned all this? You wanted to work on the film project with me?" He started to kiss me again, and it was hard to concentrate.

"That's right," he said softly. "I made sure we sat two seats apart because that's how Mr. Jordan picks the teams."

I frowned. "But you couldn't have known that Steve would steal my idea. . . ."

"I suspected it. He looks like the type who never had an idea in his life. Besides, I heard you tell him about the video game topic, and it was easy to predict the rest."

"How come I never saw what a rat he was?" I said, half to myself.

Jeff grinned and pulled me close to him. "Because you were too busy letting the stars tell you what to do. You didn't see what was right under that beautiful nose of yours."

Something was still bothering me. "And you never wanted to date Diana?"

He shook his head. "That was just a smokescreen. She was a bubblehead. Anyway, I think she and Steve are made for each other. I hope they'll be very happy. In fact, if they're lucky, they'll be as happy as you and me."

He pulled me close to kiss me again, and suddenly I forgot all about Steve and Diana.

Fifteen

"I saved some dinner for you," Mom said when I bounded into the living room.

"That's okay," I said breathlessly. I made a mad dash for the stairs. "I just have half an hour to shower and change. I've got a date tonight. With Jeff," I added happily.

"Well, that's a surprise." Mom was smiling at me. "I thought you two were just friends."

I paused on the landing. "I thought so, too, but boy was I wrong!" I darted into the bedroom and started pulling things out of my closet. I wanted to wear something special for my first real date with Jeff. I wanted to look terrific. I was holding a frilly white blouse up to me when I heard the phone ring. A moment later, Mom called up the stairs.

"It's Laura, and she said it's urgent."

I snatched the phone off the hook. "Hi Laura," I said hurriedly. "I hate to be rude, but unless this is really a matter of life and death, I need to get ready for my date —"

"It is a matter of life and death! The most wonderful thing in my whole life has just happened to me —"

"I know the feeling," I said wryly. Laura was too keyed up to notice the sarcasm in my voice: "Laura, can you kind of get on with it, because I'm really running late."

"I don't know where to start," she said helplessly. "My whole life has changed, and I just don't know how to explain it."

I glanced at my watch and sighed. Unless I stepped in, Laura would be good for half an hour. "Laura, don't try to explain it. Just tell me what happened, Just the bottom line." *And if you can do it in twenty-five words or less, so much the better,* I felt like adding.

"Okay, I'll try," she giggled. "But when you're in love, nothing makes sense, does it? Life becomes a rainbow, and there're shades and colors you've never seen before. . . ."

"Laura, please!" I pleaded.

She took a deep breath. "Okay, I'll calm down. I'll start at the beginning, like you always tell me."

"Just so it doesn't take too long," I said nervously. I started to wriggle into my jeans while I held the phone against my ear.

"Well, let me just say that the horoscope was right: Everything is written in the stars." She paused, and I guessed I was supposed to say something.

"And. . . ." I said, a little impatiently.

"And, I finally let the stars guide me. And

you'll never believe what happened!"

"Not if you don't tell me, I won't," I muttered under my breath.

"I went out with Rick Jacobs this afternoon, and I had the best time of my whole life!"

For a minute, I was too stunned to answer. The words pounded in my head, but they didn't make sense. Rick Jacobs? Best time of my life? They didn't even belong in the same sentence! "Say that again, slowly," I said.

She laughed. "I said, I went out with Rick Jacobs, and I had the best time of my life. The horoscope told me to," she said seriously. "Didn't you check your horoscope today?"

"No, I didn't have time. I've been out all day, and in fact, I'm getting ready to go out again. . . ."

Laura didn't take the hint. "Wait, I've got the paper right here."

"That's okay, I'm —"

"It's no trouble," she said merrily. "Yours says that it's a topsy-turvy day, and to expect the unexpected." She paused. "Did anything unusual happen?"

"Laura, you don't know the half of it." I couldn't keep the news to myself any longer. "I spent the whole day with Jeff, and we had a fantastic time. He wants me to go out with him, you know, to be his girlfriend, and we're going out tonight. In fact, he said we're going out every weekend night." I finally stopped to catch my breath. "It's the craziest, most wonderful thing that ever happened to me."

"So the horoscope was right," she said wonderingly. "You did have a topsy-turvy day."

"It wasn't right all along," I reminded her. "According to the stars, Steve was the right guy for me, and Jeff was the wrong guy. But then Steve stole my idea for the film project —"

"He did what?" she interrupted.

"Never mind, I don't have time to explain it," I said. "Anyway, just take my word for it. Jeff is the right boy for me, and he always has been."

"I'm convinced," she said with a laugh. "And now let me tell you my news. I finally gave in and went out with Rick Jacobs —"

"I know. I can't believe it."

"And I fell in love."

"Laura, I don't know what to say," I began. "I mean, you're my best friend, and the last thing in the world I'd want to do would be to hurt your feelings. . . ." I paused, wondering what to say next. "But you and Rick Jacobs!" I blurted out. "I just can't picture it!"

Laura laughed so hard she started choking. "Me and Rick Jacobs! No, that's not it at all." She started to say something else, and then gave in to another round of giggles.

"Well, what is it, then?" I said, more confused than ever.

"I met Rick's cousin," she finally managed

to say. "And the guy's a dream. He's taking me out to that new restaurant on the beach tonight, and then we're going dancing. Don't you see? If I hadn't listened to the horoscope, I never would have gone out with Rick, I wouldn't have met Chuck. . . ."

"And you wouldn't have had the most wonderful day of your life," I finished for her.

"Right."

For a moment, neither one of us spoke. "It could just be coincidence," I said slowly.

"It could be," she agreed. "Or there really could be something to astrology. And don't forget taseology. The tea leaves told me this would be an important day, too."

I groaned. "You're back to tea leaves."

"Well, actually, I've found something better. Do you know anything about tarot? I've been studying up on it, and there are really some amazing possibilities. I guess you know that there are seventy-eight cards, and each card has a certain meaning. . . ."

"Laura, I —"

"See, the Major Aracana cards are numbered 1 to 21, and there's a card numbered zero called The Fool. . . ."

"I really don't have time to —"

"But the really exciting part is the way you lay out the cards. You can lay them out in the portrait spread. That outlines a person's past, present, and future. . . ."

I rested the phone on the dresser and tried

on my new blouse. It looked terrific with the jeans, and I added a straw belt. Jeff would love it.

I picked up the phone. "The prediction spread is interesting," I heard Laura saying, "because it will answer a specific question. For example, you could ask if you're going to have a good time tonight. Would you like me to do a quick reading?" she offered. "It only takes a few minutes to lay out the cards, and we can do it over the phone."

"You don't need to, Laura," I told her. "Because I already know the answer. I can forecast my own future now."

"You can?"

"Yes, I can. And I'm going to make a prediction right now. I, Tracy Evans, am going to have a terrific time tonight. Not just a good time, or a nice time, but a really terrific time!"

"Well, I'm glad you feel that way," Laura said, "but it never hurts to double check. I can get the cards, and we'll —"

"I don't need the cards, or the tea leaves, or the stars anymore." I paused. "In fact, all I really need is a boy named Jeff Nichols."

"Are you sure, because —"

"I'm sure. In fact, I'm more sure than I ever have been in my whole life." I took a peek in the mirror. Not bad at all, I decided. I probably couldn't compete with the beautiful Diana, but then, come to think of it, I didn't have to. Not any more. I glanced at my watch. In just ten minutes, I'd see Jeff. I felt very happy. "Uh, Laura, I have to run now, but I'll talk to you tomorrow, okay?"

"Sure, but I really think we should take a look at the tarot cards. You never know what fate may have in store for you tonight, and —"

"Thanks anyway, but I think I know exactly what fate has in store for me."

"Are you positive?"

"I'm positive. I'll tell you all about it tomorrow, Laura."

I could feel myself smiling as I hung up.